heat

gay men
tell their
real-life
sex stories

heat

edited by
jack hart

alyson
books

LOS ANGELES • NEW YORK

© 1997 by Jack Hart. All rights reserved.

Manufactured in the United States of America.
Printed on acid-free paper.

This trade paperback original is published by Alyson Publications Inc.,
P.O. Box 4371, Los Angeles, California 90078-4371.
Distribution in the United Kingdom by Turnaround Publisher Services Ltd.,
Unit 3 Olympia Trading Estate, Coburg Road, Wood Green,
London N226TZ, England.

First edition: October 1997

01 00 99 98 97   10 9 8 7 6 5 4 3 2 1

ISBN 1-55583-435-3

CONTENTS

vi

Back in the Closet

About twenty years ago — during spring break in my last semester at college — I came home to come out to my parents. They've always been pretty liberal, so I knew there wouldn't be any hassles. And I was right. They accepted me right away, but what they did have a hard time accepting was Joey, my lover.

I insisted on bringing him down with me even though he himself was hesitant. Not only did I need him for moral support, but I also didn't think I could last two whole weeks without his luscious cock between my lips.

The night we arrived I had "the talk" with my folks. Like I said, they were really good about it until the subject of Joey came up. Actually, I think it was just a case of bad timing more than anything else. They were having a big party for my dad's boss that night at the house, and my mom was paranoid about the slightest little thing fucking it up. She asked that I keep Joey under wraps for just that one night.

Fair enough. Except just then the doorbell rang. It was my dad's boss. Before I had a chance to shoo Joey upstairs, my dad let him in. I shoved Joey into the front hall closet (so ironic) in the hope of sneaking him upstairs once I got the chance.

But I never did. More people followed, and soon our living room was filled with middle-aged execs and their harried wives.

1

jack hart

I was so busy fetching hors d'oeuvres and scotch and sodas that I completely forgot Joey was still in the closet. (I've got to tell you, he was a terrific sport about the whole mess.) Then Mrs. so-and-so gave me a coat to hang up, and when I opened the door, there I saw him, crouched between the slide projector and some hip-high fishing boots.

He grabbed me by the wrist and pulled me in, shutting the door behind us.

He was all over me in a flash. I thought he'd be angry about having to sneak around like that, but the furtiveness of it all just seemed to get him hotter and hotter. Before I knew it, my cock was out of my pants and in his mouth.

The whole time he was sucking on my rod, I could hear my parents' guests on the other side of the door. On the one hand I was terrified that someone would open the door and find this normal, middle-class college kid getting a blow job from another man. But on the other hand it was wildly exciting. Kind of like making love in a public place. In all our months together, our lovemaking had never been so frenzied.

Joey pushed me back onto the floor, and I kind of crouched against the far wall of the closet. There was no room for me to stretch my legs out, so he lifted my ankles up over his shoulders and got back to servicing my pud.

He drew the fleshy foreskin back with his teeth and nibbled on my exposed shaft. I was still in my pants, so he couldn't get all the way down to my balls. He made up for it by sucking on the head like a lollipop, which drove me absolutely nuts. He flicked his tongue around the slit and sucked up the clear pre-come that started oozing out.

The closet was too cramped for me to reciprocate, so I just lay back and slid my hands underneath my dress shirt and played with my nipples.

Joey was an expert cocksucker and knew just how to work with whatever he could get. His hot mouth engulfed the rosy head, drawing it in and out with the force of a vacuum cleaner

2

and making loud sucking and slurping noises. His rough hands roamed my ass, searching for a way to get at my crack through my slacks. But he couldn't find one, so instead he massaged the globes, circling around and around with his big palms.

I bucked my hips upward, trying to shove the whole length of my aching prick into his anxious throat, but I kept ramming him with my fly. He pushed me back down onto the floor and slowed down appreciably, taking his time to eat my cock.

I moaned softly and writhed underneath him, reaching my hands out to touch his broad shoulders (he has a great body, by the way). Instead I found his own bulging basket. Deftly I unzipped the fly and released his meat from his shorts. It was already dripping with precome. I slicked my fingers over its surface and began to pump him with all my might.

We would have been quite a sight had anyone opened the closet door at that very moment: Joey hanging over me, my six-inch cock stuffed deep into his mouth, my hands filled with his big throbbing piece.

We wanted to bring each other off simultaneously — we had never been able to do that before — so we kind of kept each other in check. I'd slow down, and he'd slow down. I'd pick up the pace, and he'd follow. Soon we were in perfect rhythm with each other. I couldn't even tell if the hot moans and groans were coming from him or from me.

Then we both felt it at the same time: that familiar rush of hot juice swirling around in our nuts and then making that final journey up our shafts. I just wished that my lips were clamped down around Joey's big, juicy cock so that I could taste his jizz shooting out.

He swallowed all of me and then licked my pole dry. I settled for the next best thing: I caught as much of his juice as I could in my hand and stuffed my fingers into my mouth, licking them clean like a kid licking the pudding bowl.

We stuffed our limp dicks back into our pants and tried to catch our breath. Then, like a secret spy in enemy territory, I

3

jack hart

sneaked out of the closet and joined my parents in the living room. Nobody had even missed me.

At the first chance I had, I whisked Joey out of the closet and up to my bedroom.

Later that night my parents saw that my bedroom light was on and asked Joey down to join us. They were afraid he might have been bored all night.

God, I hope not.

Lifesaver

It had always been my dream to be a lifeguard, so I spent a lot of time swimming to build up endurance. As the summer season drew closer, I enrolled in a CPR class at the YMCA to round out my training.

When I arrived at the Y, I headed straight for the pool. No one else was around except for a lean, gorgeous man standing at the far end of the pool. I hoped he was my instructor.

He was. His name was Peter. He was in his early thirties, stood about five feet ten inches tall, and had black hair and deep blue eyes surrounded by long black lashes. Solid, well-defined muscles and a taut chest and stomach gave the look of a boxer.

We went through about an hour of basics, and Peter demonstrated the technique on Dead Donna, the mannequin. It was a little hard practicing on a dummy because I couldn't really tell if I was doing it right. So Peter decided to let me have a go at a live person — him.

He lay down on the tile floor and closed his eyes. I noticed that his pecker was getting a little full, but it was still a long way from hard. Still, it was a good five inches. I bent down, tilted his head back, plugged his nose, and blew, but his tongue blocked his throat. I covered his mouth with mine again and pushed my tongue as far as I could, but he wouldn't budge. My tongue became an assault weapon, poking and prodding his mouth.

5

jack hart

Out of the corner of my eye I saw his full masculinity rise to the occasion, about ten and a half inches! With my next thrust his tongue came alive, reaching into my mouth and exploring.

He grabbed my shoulders like a vise and rolled me over onto my back. Pinned by this hunk, I couldn't move except in rhythm with his body grinding into mine. His mouth was suddenly everywhere: over my eyes, ears, nose, and throat.

Slowly he worked his way down and around my body, using only his mouth to guide him. He tongued my armpits and chewed on my nipples. He moved from my tits down along my stomach and into my belly button, where he ran into the fine line of hair leading to my crotch. He chewed all the way down until he came to the bush of pubic hair. He investigated it with his tongue and without warning took my entire seven-and-a-half-incher into his mouth.

I started trembling all over and felt my cock pulsating. He mumbled, "Not yet," and went to work on my tight scrotum. Both my balls were in his mouth, and he gargled with them, sending spasms from the base of my spine up through my neck.

He dropped between my legs and started licking me like an all-day sucker. With each stroke of his tongue my pecker responded. I opened my legs wider and arched my back involuntarily. The tip of his tongue found my glory hole. He hoisted my legs over his wide shoulders and assaulted my love button. I had never experienced such an incredible feeling. He started licking down the insides of my legs until he reached my feet. He gave each of my toes a blow job.

After that he whispered that he wanted me to fuck him. He rolled over onto his back with his knees bent. Next he grabbed my meat and guided it in. This was my first full-blown sexual experience, and I can't describe the feeling of having my love tool squeezed inside a warm body.

After only a few strokes I shot my load with such force that I thought all my insides were draining. After my spasms subsided, Peter reached down, squeezed his ass, and bucked. He breathed hard and shot a load of come all over his chest and stomach. I bent down and licked it off. Then we hit the showers and scrubbed each other down.

I went on to become a pretty good lifeguard.

Good Neighbor Max

When I was thirty years old, I had a small studio apartment in SoHo, New York's downtown arts district. The rent was high, and the neighborhood looked like a demilitarized zone. But the neighbors were great.

Especially Max, who lived in the same building. I visited with him almost daily: We shared a lot of the same interests and got along well. Though I was pretty sure Max was straight, I secretly harbored a crush on him from the day I first saw him.

He was twenty-eight years old, stood five feet eleven inches tall, and weighed a solid 150 pounds. He had a slight but well-defined build. He worked out three times a week, and his body really showed it. Aside from his boyish charm and stunning bleached-blond looks, the thing that attracted me most to Max was his warm personality.

One hot summer day I dropped in at Max's place just as he was leaving. He was going jogging and suggested I hang around till he got back. Neither of us had eaten lunch yet, so we planned on going out for a bite when he returned.

I waited for him to come back — trying to keep myself preoccupied with some daytime talk shows on TV — but I just couldn't get my mind off Max's running around outside in his tight little nylon shorts. Just thinking of him getting all hot and sweaty started to make me horny as hell.

By the time he got back, he was soaked with perspiration. His shorts clearly outlined his hefty bulge and tight little ass, and his T-shirt clung to his finely etched pecs. I could see that his nipples were erect and straining against the cotton. He told me he was going to shower and change and that we'd be leaving in a few minutes.

After a bit, Max called out to me from his bedroom. He said he wanted to show me something. With my heart pounding I approached his door, wondering what it could be. I'm sure he knew I was attracted to him, yet it didn't seem to make him uncomfortable like some other straight guys I've known.

When I entered Max's room he told me to shut the door and come over to where he was standing. I crossed the room and stood directly in front of him. Max smiled at me, and I smiled back — half out of nervousness and half out of being so close to this magnificent hunk. He was still in his workout clothes. It was too much for me: I put my hands on his chest as he looked into my eyes and told me, "Go ahead."

I hugged him tentatively, shivering in anticipation of getting to savor his entire body.

He pulled off his T-shirt, exposing nipples that begged to be sucked. I bent down and started lapping at his chest, eager to arouse this man I'd dreamed about for so long.

Max put his hands on the top of my head and gently pushed me downward. I was face-to-face with his hot crotch. As if he knew what I was thinking, he thrust his pelvis into my face and rubbed his basket all over my nose and chin.

I reached up and pulled down his shorts, exposing a jockstrap brimming with the most beautiful bulge I'd ever seen. I kissed the pouch and ran my tongue along the insides of his thighs.

He spread his legs wider, and I thought I might come just from sheer anticipation. I pulled his jockstrap down to his knees and took his hardening penis in my hands. He was breathing heavily as I wrapped my lips around the head and sucked with all my might.

jack hart

While I ate his big rubbery cock, Max rubbed his balls gently and moaned. Knowing he was getting close to shooting, Max pulled me off my knees and laid me on the bed. He straddled me, stroking his dick and fondling his balls. I gobbled down his tool, sucking harder and faster. He went wild when I began pinching his brown nipples and started to fuck my face at break-neck speed.

Precome was dribbling down my chin. I scooped it up with my fingers, reluctant to let any of this man's juice escape. Then he exploded, and I felt rapid jets of jism flooding out of the tip of his cock. This man had gallons of juice stored up in those bull balls of his.

He collapsed on top of me, and I wrapped my arms around him and whispered a thanks in his ear.

He had made my dream come true, but I'm sure he must have wished upon a star himself the night before.

Pumping Irony

As a physical education assistant here at the university, I spend a good deal of my time in the locker room putting clean towels in the baskets, picking up after the students, or whatever. In the weight room I replace barbells in the racks and supervise lifts so no one breaks his back.

There's always a fresh supply of cute, young muscular studs around to inspire my lustful daydreams. I have to be discreet when checking out the merchandise in the showers, but our locker room has large mirrors ideally situated for checking out the shiny, soapy bodies.

The weight room is better for watching the studs because it has two mirrored walls, and bodybuilders are accustomed to having their physiques admired.

One morning last week I hungrily watched an incredible guy working out in a pair of shiny electric-blue running shorts. He strained against steel to work his biceps, triceps, pecs, and lats, each rep further defining those bulging muscles.

When he straddled the weight bench to do bench presses, his bulging jock showed clearly under his thin nylon shorts. I offered to spot him, and to my delight he accepted with a wide grin. As I moved behind the barbell, I caught the warm, masculine fragrance of his body. He closed his eyes and began doing reps. I noticed excitedly that his nipples were hard.

11

jack hart

When he was done he was eager to return the favor. I lay down and "accidentally" brushed my fingertips across his crotch, as if I had missed the bar. I looked up and mumbled an apology, but he was smiling.

I slid my head up closer to his crotch and smelled the sexy aroma of his cock. I pushed myself to do a few extra reps and then said, "Time to hit the showers."

As I stopped to get a drink of water on the way to the showers, I saw him exit behind me. His locker wasn't near mine, so I pulled off my shorts and lay down on the bench, hoping to catch a glimpse of him in the mirror. I heard him padding toward me on bare feet, so I stood up, my back to him, and slowly pulled down my jock. I could see him approaching in the mirror.

Sending him a piercing stare and inviting smile, I wrapped my towel around my neck and chose the farthest shower from the door, knowing that he was following.

He moved into the shower next to mine and began lathering his chest. Turning away, he soaped his ass and crotch. I made no attempt to hide my growing hard-on as I stepped over to him and began lathering his back.

Reaching up to grasp the shower head with my hands, I heard a low moan escape his lips. I worked my way down to his ass. My fully erect nine-and-a-half-inch cock ached to get between those ass cheeks, so I pulled him closer as I inserted my cock between his thighs. I fondled his thick, hard cock and swollen balls and slowly started jacking him off with my right hand as my left squeezed his balls.

Varying the tempo, I kept us both on the verge of orgasm for as long as I could stand it. Then, using some of his cream rinse as a lubricant, I penetrated his hot, tight asshole with the head of my cock. Manipulating his hard nipples with one hand, I continued to jerk him off with the other as I eased my hard, throbbing love rod into his hot ass.

Aching for release, we both quivered in agony and ecstasy as I pulled out and thrust in again with increasing tempo. He met

12

my thrusts with his own and a tightening of his ass muscles. Then he reached the final crest and shot off spurt after spurt of hot, creamy come in my hand. At almost the same time I exploded in fiery eruptions.

Disentangling ourselves, we then finished our shower. As we dried off and dressed, we made small talk. His name was Ross. He'd been coming to the gym for a few months — ironically, just to meet me.

With a parting kiss and a squeeze of my ass, he left.

He eventually left the university, but he comes back quite often for our own special reunions.

The Element of Surprise

When I was in the Air Force, I found myself on the duty end of a flashlight as barracks patrol just about as often as the next guy. One difference was, whereas other guys bitched about having to patrol the barracks, I found a way to make the job one that I thoroughly enjoyed.

By the time I had my first experience with male lust, I was still a virgin; I hadn't even had a woman. The man who caught my eye was a really well-built guy from my home state. He was housed in my barracks, so I could watch him all the time. He had broad shoulders and a beefy chest covered with thick brown hair. He couldn't have been more than twenty-four years old, and he was very friendly.

One night around 2 a.m., while making the obligatory rounds in the barracks, I spotted him sprawled out across his bunk, wearing only his white skivvies, which were barely covering an obvious bulge. Lying there, asleep, he looked like a god.

His muscular, hairy legs were spread invitingly, and I let a ray of light from my flashlight glide across his chest. I knelt beside the bunk and lightly touched his thigh. It was smooth and taut, hard as granite.

Afraid I would wake him, I continued on my rounds, but I couldn't forget the image of his terrific body. At the 3 a.m. pass-through, I went straight to his bunk. His was still asleep, but his cock was erect. The head peeked precariously from the tight waistband, a drop of precome glistening in the gaping eye.

One arm was raised behind his head; the other was folded across his stomach. One leg was arched up; the other, straight.

Again I knelt beside the bunk, my head dangerously close to his chest. His nipples were large and flat, almost hidden beneath the circles of curly hair. His handsome face relaxed in repose as he slept deeply. I wanted to touch the slowly pulsing cock, but, fearful of awakening him, I just leaned close to his body — near enough to feel the brush of chest hair against my cheek. He stirred slightly, and his hand dipped into the waistband of his shorts and grasped his thick tool.

He stroked it slowly, and I watched as it grew. A full three inches now protruded from the band of his shorts, and his fingers laced the lower shaft.

I laid down the flashlight and allowed my hand to rest ever so lightly on his hairy stomach. I could feel the warmth of his manhood. I was again taken with the incredible beauty of those powerful legs as he raised first one and then the other. After straightening them out again, his hips rose against the pressure of his handful of cock.

I eased a finger beneath the waistband and pulled his shorts slowly downward, just until his huge balls fell into view. He shrugged and moved his hand away, running it up his chest and resting it near his neck.

His body lay before me in naked glory. The soft light of the flashlight glowed in the darkness, emphasizing the muscular contours of his chest. I could smell his freshly showered body.

The thick vein beneath the shaft of his cock throbbed in the light, and I touched the heavy-hanging balls. He didn't move as my hand caressed the soft firmness.

Unable to contain my desire any longer, I placed my tongue flat against the tumescent shaft and trailed it slowly upward along the pulsating vein. God, it tasted good. He stirred, and I ducked down beside the bunk.

jack hart

He turned onto his side, facing me, and his cock fell invitingly across his thigh. Easing back up to the side of the bunk, I slowly licked his spongy cock head and in seconds had its fullness between my anxious lips.

I sucked slowly and deliberately on the delicate morsel of flesh. I heard him moaning deep in his throat, and I pushed more thick inches into my mouth until I had taken half of his cock. I eased back to the head, then down again, until I could feel his crotch hair rubbing my nose.

I could feel his cock expanding against my tongue. I circled the swollen knob and then pushed downward again. I felt his hand touching the back of my head and pulling me forward, thrusting the entire length of his cock deep into my throat. I almost gagged, but I managed to ease back just enough to allow myself some breathing room. Reluctantly I eased the massive tool from my lips and looked at his face.

His eyes were closed, and a smile graced his handsome face. His hairy chest heaved more quickly. My tongue caressed his heavy nuts — softly, gently — and then returned to his wet bulbous cock head. I opened my mouth, and his hips pushed forward, sinking the delectable firmness between my jaws again.

My hand roamed over his thighs and legs, then grasped his warm, smooth ass cheeks as I pulled him closer. His cock slipped deeper into my throat, and he groaned and lay back again, his broad chest looking like a Greek god's in the soft light of the first dawn.

I sucked his cock steadily, running my lips around the head and shaft, until his quivering thighs signaled the first burst of thick white come across my spiraling tongue.

He never woke up — at least, I never thought he did. And he never mentioned what happened. If he knew I was the one who had given him head, he never let on, and we never shared the experience again.

Boathouse Rock

I am thirty-three years old and the department head at a very large advertising agency in Detroit. At six feet four, I am tall and lean. I weigh an impressive 210 heavily muscled pounds. My weight-trained body is in peak condition, hard and muscular. Be it in the exercise room at home or at the corporate health club, I spend many hours three times a week pumping iron to maintain the toned body I developed many years ago while playing football in college (before a knee injury ended my hopes of a career in the pros). My broad shoulders and 46-inch chest narrow to an almost too-small 31-inch waist and slim hips. My arms and legs bulge with tight, rippling muscles, as do my well-shaped buttocks. What little body hair I have does not obscure the effective display of my body's powerful muscle mass. Because of my ruggedly handsome face, strong jawline, slightly cleft chin, deep cobalt-blue eyes, killer smile, and long, thick, curly almost-black hair, many people who meet me for the first time assume that I am a male model and tell me that I look like a modern-day Hercules.

This past summer I took several vacation days and drove to northern Michigan, where my wealthy parents own a cottage on three acres of lakefront land. Having the whole place to myself, I sunbathed in the nude on their private dock beside the boathouse they had built behind the cottage.

jack hart

On my fourth day there, I looked up while sunbathing and noticed a very good-looking hazel-eyed, blond-haired man in his late twenties, wearing a black Speedo and leather sandals, approaching me through the woods from the neighboring cottage. Although I had met him only once before, I quickly recognized him. He was the son-in-law of the couple who owned the cottage next door.

"Hi, guy," he said, smiling, as he approached the dock. "I saw your Porsche in the driveway as we drove in yesterday, so, needing to get away from the nagging wife and screaming kids for a few minutes, I thought I would stop over for a small chat." He walked up to me and extended his hand. "Are you here with your parents?"

"Hi," I replied. "No, I'm here alone." I reached my hand out and took his in a handshake. Since I was lying on my stomach and he was obviously straight — being married with children — I didn't bother covering my nude body from his view with the towel I had. "There's a refrigerator in the boathouse," I said. "Why don't you grab us a couple of beers?"

When he returned and handed me a beer, I rolled over onto my side and sat up on one elbow. His eyes quickly fell to my crotch and took in my well-trimmed pubic bush and the way my thick nine-inch uncircumcised cock and large, cleanly shaved balls flopped over my muscular thigh and rested on the wooden dock I was lying on. I thought I also could detect a hint of lust in his exploring eyes.

"I didn't know anyone was around," I offered. "I often sunbathe in the nude. I hope you don't mind." As I smiled at him, I noticed a telltale bulge growing in his swimsuit.

"Not at all," he stammered. "If I was hung like you are, I'd be naked all the time."

His eyes continued to be locked on my crotch. His surprising interest in my anatomy was having its effect on me as well. No matter how hard I tried to stop it from happening, I was starting to sprout a hard-on!

18

Trying to ignore my obvious arousal, I talked about sports, cars, sailing, anything! We talked for about twenty minutes. His eyes never left my swelling cock and balls.

"You're burning," he said all of a sudden, grabbing my bottle of tanning lotion and moving behind me. "Let me put some of this sunblock on your back."

At that moment I knew something very erotic was going to happen between us.

He gently massaged the lotion onto my back. He was kneeling so close to me that I could feel his breath on the back of my shoulder.

"Since I have my hands wet with lotion, I might as well finish the job," he said as his hands moved along the back of my hairy legs.

My cock throbbed to full erection!

His hands moved up my hard-muscled legs and attacked my muscular buttocks. Before I could protest, his fingers slid into the hairy crack of my ass and began teasing my quivering asshole. I moaned helplessly. His fingers quickly left my ass, only to slide between my thighs and massage my heavy balls and pulsing cock.

"Not here," I said in a heated whisper. "Let's go inside the boathouse."

Once inside, he quickly dropped to his knees and started sucking my aching cock. His hands were all over my body, pinching my nipples, groping my ass cheeks, probing a finger in my asshole, pulling on my balls, rubbing my thighs. He pulled his mouth off my towering cock and started mouthing my swelling balls. He jacked his fist along my blood-engorged prick as he licked my fat nuts. He couldn't seem to get enough of my muscle-packed body! When he tired of sucking my balls, he ran his head between my thighs, tonguing my ass crack and rimming my twitching asshole.

I pushed him away from me and nearly ripped his swimsuit from his body, revealing his thick forest of blond pubic hair, erect seven-inch circumcised cock — which was dripping with precome — and large, hairy balls. I pushed him to the floor, and we quickly got into a sixty-nine position, sucking each other's cock until we both shot our respective loads.

After a short rest he lifted his legs in the air and begged me to fuck his ass. He didn't have to ask twice. It was a long, violent fuck; he wanted it to be brutal. I usually don't go for that type of scene, but he pleaded for me to rape his asshole. I gave him every inch of my long, fat tool in deep lunges.

We spent the next two hours sucking and fucking in the boathouse. We would have been at it all afternoon had he not noticed the time on the clock on the wall. Not wanting his wife to come over looking for him and find him there with me, he quickly slipped on his swimsuit and sandals and left.

Needless to say, he returned later that night after his wife had fallen asleep. He sneaked into my bedroom and crawled into my bed. I awoke to find him sucking on my big cock!

He and his family live about twelve miles from my home in the suburbs of Detroit, so he and I have continued our affair. I know he will never leave his wife and children for me — and I don't want him to. I enjoy our purely physical sexual relationship. I still have my freedom!

Morning Show

Several years ago I lived on the fourth floor of a Portland, Oregon, apartment building. I liked the area and had a good view of foot traffic on N.W. 21st Street. Directly across the street was the bus stop, and standing there one morning was a man I estimated to be about twenty-five years old. He was wearing well-worn blue jeans, which showed a particularly large bulge. He definitely had my attention when the damned bus suddenly arrived and swept him up. *Oh, well, once again left high and dry,* I thought.

Not to be left holding a raging hard-on, I continued my surveillance of the street below for another suitable visual aid to enhance my release. Apparently I was not the only person who was so inspired by the young man at the bus stop. One floor below mine in the building next door was the catch of the day. He had a small room, which he used as a breakfast nook, that looked out over the street. Most mornings he was dressed and ready for work, reading the newspaper in a general rush. Today he was seated at the table in his bathrobe, casually stroking one of the most beautiful cocks I've ever seen. His interest was obviously centered on the street below. As the daily stream of men came into view, his excitement increased, and his determination to climax became evident. As they passed by he eased up and went back to his newspaper. He was driving me absolutely wild.

21

jack hart

Here I was, in broad daylight, stark naked, with a true bird's-eye view of this fantastic stud beating his meat.

How, I asked myself, *do I get his attention without scaring him off?* I figured that if he liked what he saw on the street, he would like what he could see in my window. With that in mind I waited for the best moment to make my move. After a time he modestly pulled his robe closed and returned to his newspaper. At that I threw open my window — taking pains to create as much racket as possible — and took a long, slow stretch as I gazed off into the distance. Then I walked away from that window and went to another window, where I peeked out to see if I had attracted any interest.

Bingo! I thought. *I have his attention.* I returned to the first window once again and allowed one hand to rub ever so casually across my chest. After a second or two, I lowered my other hand to my crotch and groped my cock in what I hoped would appear to be an absentminded fashion. Slowly I began to pay more attention to my cock and worked myself up into a nice, slow stroke session.

Without looking directly at my neighbor's window, I could still detect movement peripherally. Once again he was stroking his meat. Dropping my head along with my pretense, I stared directly into his eyes with a warm smile. We were both cool with the situation.

Feeling concerned that others might be able to see me, I backed away from the window. To hold my attention, he got up out of his chair and lay flat on the floor, affording me a full view of his body. After a leisurely round of tit twisting, cock stroking, and squirming on the floor, he left for a moment, only to return with his telephone number scrawled boldly on a piece of paper. With an invitation like that, how could I resist?

We chatted briefly on the phone, making remarks like "Nice cock" and "Wanna fuck?" Before we hung up I gave him my apartment number, and he hurried right over. Once he was safely inside my apartment, it was, so to speak, no "holes" barred. I

22

undressed my prize and fell to my knees, taking his entire eight inches in one great swallow. This was fantasy at its best.

"Chuck's the name, and fucking's the game," he said as he pulled me to my feet, spun me around, and pressed his big uncut cock against my willing asshole. Like lightning from a far-off thundercloud, he struck with a vengeance, piercing me with pleasure, pumping me with passion. We finally shot our loads at the same time in a feverish rush — mine all over the floor, his all over my back — and then we collapsed together in a sweaty, breathless tangle.

Needless to say, this activity became a fairly regular morning ritual for us.

I eventually moved away from Portland, but I never lost Chuck's phone number. Whenever I go back there, we get together in his breakfast nook and watch "breakfast snacks" walk the streets below. We always have our cocks in our hands and our heads held high. We never know when we might have a chance meeting with a like-minded gentleman living, as I once did, on the fourth floor.

A Married Man

About a week and a half ago, a friend of mine, Rick, called and asked if he could sleep on my couch. His wife had just thrown him out. To make a long story short, he informed me of all the details of the separation, and I agreed to have him as my guest for a few days. I kept reminding myself it was going to be just a temporary inconvenience.

Sharing my small apartment was more difficult than I had imagined it would be. Rick was perfectly comfortable walking around in his tight-fitting Jockeys or even naked after taking a shower, but having him hanging around in such a state made me distinctly uncomfortable. Rick is thirty-five, dark, hairy, and very handsome. Regular workouts have definitely paid off. It was all I could do to conceal my excitement as my rock-hard cock strained against my jeans.

Friday night Rick came home to my apartment after working out at the gym. Being all hot and sweaty, he headed straight for the shower. He left the door to the bathroom halfway open, so I was able to hear the water running. This brought a burning image of Rick into my mind — of his standing under the steamy spray in all his nakedness, soaping up his big cock and balls. The thought was more than I could take.

When I heard the water shut off, I got up from my seat on the couch and went to see if I could get a better look. I saw Rick get out of the shower and start to dry himself off in front of the bathroom mirror. He must have been horny too, because I saw his cock grow to its full nine inches while he was toweling himself off. Then he dropped his towel and began to stroke his veiny dick while he cupped his hairy, low-hanging balls with the other hand. He closed his eyes for a second while his fist began to pump faster.

I knew I shouldn't be watching, but I was unable to take my eyes off my buddy while he stood there playing with his big dick. He must have sensed my presence because he swung the door open, and we were suddenly face-to-face. "What the fuck are you doing?" he demanded as he grabbed me by my shirt. I thought for sure I was dead meat until he yanked my shirt off and, before I knew it, had my shorts pulled down too. He sat down on the toilet and forced me, bare-assed, over his knees. He reached for the hairbrush on the sink and said I needed to be punished. I don't know if I was scared or just excited.

I'd never been spanked before, but I obviously found it arousing because, as Rick paddled my butt, my cock started growing, pressing against Rick's stomach. All I could do was moan as my ass reddened and grew hot. Rick kept saying he was going to teach me a lesson I would never forget. While I was bent over him, he spread my legs farther apart. My ass was so fucking on fire that I begged him to stop. I reached down between his legs and stroked his cock, which he didn't seem to mind.

After my spanking Rick had me get on all fours and spread my legs wide. With a little lube Rick worked both of his thumbs into my hot, tight asshole. It hurt at first, but then my ass adjusted to his thick fingers. He kept working his thumbs into my hole, twisting and prodding, saying he wanted to open me up so I could take his big dick. I didn't need any coaxing. My ass was so hot and wet that I begged him for another finger; he obliged at once. I thought I would go crazy being finger-fucked by this Italian stud. I saw him reach for some lube and put some on his big purple meat, which he plunged deep into my ass.

jack hart

I yelled, but Rick didn't slow down. Although my ass was still red from the spanking, he continued slapping my cheeks as he rammed his hard meat into me. I was so aroused that I had to jack myself off. Precome was already oozing out of my dick. Meanwhile, Rick's cock had become so engorged, I felt certain he would split me in two. Dripping with sweat, he spread my cheeks as wide as they would go and pounded me with such force, his balls were slapping my ass with every thrust.

What with the feeling of his cock burying itself in my butt, the sound of our flesh smacking together, and the sight of Rick crouching over me in the mirror, I was being pushed over the edge. I slowed up on my own cock to make the moment last. Rick could tell by my moans that I was close to coming, so he picked up the pace as he slammed his meat into my chute. He reached around in front of me and grabbed my balls, squeezing them almost to the point of pain. I thought he was going to milk my load right out of me.

He began to yank his cock all the way out of me and then ram it all the way back in with each thrust. It was all I could take, and with one final squeeze of his hand on my balls, I began to unload. Come exploded from my dick and shot halfway across the room, puddling on the floor. Rick kept pounding my tight ass, so I clamped it even tighter around his cock. "Oh, shit!" he moaned. "I'm coming!" I felt his hot jizz shoot up my hole and thought he'd never stop. When he pulled out, my ass was dripping with his load. It took us a few minutes to catch our breath.

We carried on for at least half the night. Never would I have imagined my married friend to be so kinky. I know one thing for sure: He had very little spare time to ponder his estranged wife. Needless to say, Rick moved from my couch to my water bed. Now the phrases "Surf's up" and "Riding the waves" have entirely new meanings for me.

26

Auto Sex

I remember jacking off in front of a mirror ever since I was twelve years old, but it's only since the AIDS crisis that I've developed my self-love fantasy into an art form. I still have occasional safer-sex encounters with friends or new acquaintances, but more and more I enjoy the idea of spending time at home alone in front of my two full-length mirrors.

Often I'll be changing clothes after work or getting ready to take a shower, and I'll catch a glimpse of myself in the mirror. The sight of my hairless white ass and smooth swimmer's build instantly turns me on, and for a second I'll stand there breathless, admiring myself, my cock quickly stiffening.

It's not that I'm the hottest guy in the world, though people do think I'm good-looking, even cute. I'm five foot ten, weigh 160 pounds, and work out regularly. I'm twenty-seven years old, but I'm taken for twenty-two or twenty-three all the time.

There are plenty of guys I find as attractive as myself, if not more so; it's just that the idea of a guy's turning on to his own body has always seemed so hot to me.

I especially like stripping slowly in front of a mirror. I make sure there's enough light to see my entire body clearly. I pump up my chest and arms and then turn to the side to admire my ass. I love looking at the crack and fantasizing what it would be like to lick it myself. I carefully feel my ass with one hand and reach with the other in between the cheeks to my asshole. By now my prick is fully engorged, and I am stroking it feverishly.

27

jack hart

Often I will have worked out at the gym earlier in the day, and I'll have purposely not showered so that the smell of my sweat-covered asshole will be strong. Standing in front of the mirror, I press the fingers of one hand directly onto my asshole, rubbing it, massaging it. As I watch myself beating off, I bring my hand up so I can smell my ass-scented fingers. The idea of a hot guy smelling his own ass is an unbelievable turn-on to me. And the idea of a guy actually wanting to rim his own ass — or fantasizing about it — is enough to make me shoot my wad. I lick my fingers to taste my own ass, then repeat the ritual several times, pulling back each time just before I come.

Sometimes I sit naked on the carpet, facing myself in the mirror, which extends completely to the floor. I raise my legs up, spread them wide, and then just stare at my hairless asshole for ten to fifteen minutes at a time, often not even masturbating. I fall into a trance as my tongue licks the air, and I dream that my face is deep between my own ass cheeks. The boldness of my self-love fantasy only turns me on more.

Sometimes I'll stand over a smaller mirror, measuring about three feet square, and look at my ass while I'm beating off in front of the larger mirror. I'll slowly lower myself onto the smaller mirror, squatting so I can see my pink hole fully. I spread my buns and sit squarely on the mirror, as if two guys were rubbing assholes together. Precome appears at the top of my dick, and I lift it to my mouth. But I pull back again from exploding my load.

I get on all fours, doggy-style, with my ass facing the larger mirror. I place the smaller one opposite the other so that it is near my face and I can see the reflection of my ass. On the smaller mirror, where I have been sitting, I can see the sweaty outline of my asshole. I move my face closer to the outline.

I can actually smell my own ass on the glass.

I lick the ass sweat from the mirror. By now I can't hold back, and I let go. My cock shoots load after load of hot come into my hand. As my boner finishes spurting, I stand up in front of the

28

larger mirror, place my come-filled hand at face level, and slowly lick up every drop. I stare into my eyes and savor each glorious moment.

In the Navy

This is a true story, although I've changed all the names to protect the innocent — and the not-so-innocent. It begins in September 1967, when I was in the Navy.

I was ordered to the USS *Kittyhawk* for a two-year tour. I was 35-year-old lieutenant, assigned as the electronics material officer. The first few weeks were hectic with underway training and preparing to deploy for West Pac — the Gulf of Tonkin. I shared a stateroom with a wonderful pilot, Jack Thompson, and had a crackerjack master chief petty officer named Altman working for me in the office. Somehow, Altman managed to keep me out of trouble during those early days in San Diego.

After a day or two at sea, I walked out of the EMO's office, which is located on Level O3, and entered Admiral's Country. Outside the admiral's door stood a marine guard, a god, a *David*. I said to myself, *Oh no!* I knew what I was and had fought it for many years, and here standing before me was the handsomest man I had ever seen in my life.

During the next several weeks I often saw him standing at parade rest in front of that door. The name tag on his chest read J. FRASIER. One day he snapped to attention, popped a salute, and said, "Good morning, Lt. Dietrich." I returned his salute and asked how he knew my name. He replied that he had asked the guys who cleaned the passage each morning (OE Division cleaned both the admiral's and captain's passages). I asked him, "Now that you know my name, what does the *J* stand for?" He replied, "Jerry, sir!"

At 11 o'clock one night I found that I just couldn't get to sleep, so I went to my office to get some paperwork done. As I went up the admiral's passage, I noticed that Jerry was on duty. God, he was beautiful in that tight-fitting, starched, pressed uniform. And, of course, since he was standing at parade rest, his basket was really bulging.

Once in my office, I couldn't concentrate on work. All I could think about was that smile and those eyes. Suddenly I was startled by a light knock. I told whoever it was to come in, and to my surprise, in walked Jerry. He pulled the door shut and leaned against the bulkhead with his hand on the doorknob, as if he might want to get out in a hurry. I motioned for him to have a seat. Though he sat down, he acted as if the chair might be mined and ready to detonate. After a moment he asked, "What's the matter, can't you sleep on this noisy bucket?" Those were the first words he'd spoken to me outside the line of duty. I looked into those beautiful blue eyes, which tonight seemed to reflect a hint of sadness. Finally I said, "Sleeplessness has been somewhat of a problem of late."

Jerry relaxed a little. He slumped down in the chair, spread his sexy legs, and clasped his hands together behind his head. His eyes never left mine. He had changed into fatigues, and even though they were baggy in comparison to his dress uniform, that formidable bulge was still readily visible down his right leg. "When I can't sleep, I try to find a quiet, secluded place and jack off!" he said, shocking me. "Nothing works better for me." A slight smile rose at the right side of his mouth as he saw my uneasiness. I had flushed red.

He reached down with his right hand and gave his cock a pull. He was beginning to harden. I was wearing wash khakis with Jockey shorts, and my cock was pushed under my balls. I was starting to harden, and, of course, there were a few hairs under

31

my foreskin, and I was really beginning to get uncomfortable. I squirmed in my chair, trying to untangle the hair without pulling on my crotch. Finally I stood up and walked toward the door. "I think this conversation between us is out of line," I said. "It's best if you leave so I can get this paperwork done." My attempt to sound authoritarian fell flat; all I wanted was to grab him up in my arms and kiss those beautiful, full lips. He reached up, grabbed my hand, and placed it on the shaft of his rigid cock. "Jerry, what the hell do you think you're doing!"

"I'm doing to you what I've wanted to do since the first day I saw you come out of your office," he said. "And I know you want me just as much."

He reached up and began to loosen my belt. I made a feeble attempt to stop him, but he shook off my hands, pulled down the zipper, and yanked my pants to my knees. He lightly kissed the bulge in my Jockeys while gently pulling them down over my ass, making sure to keep my cock completely covered. I was so shocked at what was happening, I began to lose my erection (getting caught, being court-martialed, and losing my career all flashed through my mind). But all I did was stand there and let him do with me as he wished. Jerry gently pulled my shorts down over my crotch and lifted my cock out. "Oh, my God, you've got skin!" he whispered. He put the head of my flaccid dick in his mouth, pushing his tongue under the foreskin. He began to roll that hot tongue of his between the skin and head of my dick. After a few licks I was hard again. Then he swooped down and swallowed my fat eight-incher to the hilt.

With his powerful sucking, I was sure I would come in a few seconds. So I grabbed him by the shoulders and lifted him off my cock. (With the other hand I reached over and snapped the lock on the office door. I was praying that Master Chief Altman wouldn't come down to the office.) I squatted down, grabbed Jerry by the seat of his pants, and buried my face in his crotch, which was still covered. With shaking hands I unbuckled his belt and undid the buttons of his fatigues. He was wearing no shorts, and as I opened his pants, I was overcome by the aroma of his manly body. I pulled his pants on down those muscular legs and watched the most beautiful cock I have ever seen snap to attention in front of my face. I took the fat mushroom-headed thing into my mouth. Jerry began thrusting his pelvis in and out. "Eat it, Lieutenant Dietrich!" he demanded. And eat it I did! I was able to take a deep breath, and to my amazement I didn't gag. His thrusts got deeper, then suddenly, after only a few seconds, he went rigid and doused the back of my throat with a massive, pulsing orgasm. I continued to take the head of his cock in and out of my mouth. He pleaded for me to stop, but I refused because I didn't want it to ever end. It was my first cock, my first time to eat a man's come.

I stood up and took his face in my hands. "Jerry Frasier, may I kiss you?"

He replied, "I'm not a marine who says, 'Fuck me, but don't kiss me, 'cause kissing is queer!' Yes, you can kiss me!"

I gently forced my tongue into his mouth and lathed his tongue with mine.

Jerry took off the rest of his clothes and told me to do the same. I obeyed as ordered. He said, "Now I am going to try and suck your cock the way you did mine, and when it's hard, I want your big officer cock up my ass! I've had my finger and many other things up my ass when I jerk off, but now I want to know what it's like to have a cock up my ass."

It was obvious that Jerry was not a cocksucker because he could take barely more than the head before the gag reflex took over. But soon I was as rigid as a board and ready for action. Jerry released my cock, sat down, rolled onto his back, and said, "Please, Lieutenant Dietrich, fuck me."

I lifted his legs over my shoulders, spat in my hand, and rubbed my cock. I placed the head on his pucker and eased down. As I applied more pressure, the head slipped into the tightest confines I could imagine. Jerry sucked in his breath. I fucked him like a madman — on my knees, on my tiptoes —

and too soon came over the top. Jerry exploded for a second time and said in a whisper, "Now I really am!"

The next morning I went down to the ward room for breakfast, ate, tasted nothing, talked, said nothing, listened, heard nothing, and went to quarters for muster feeling absolutely scared to death. Master Chief Altman said nothing, not even with his eyes. That afternoon I left my office and passed the guard outside the admiral's quarters. A friend of Jerry's by the name of Keith was on duty. He grabbed my arm and said, "Did you hear about Jerry?" He told me that Jerry had awakened the marine captain early that morning and told him he was queer and was having an affair with a ship's company officer. He refused to implicate anyone. Jerry was gone on the early-morning COD and left not a word. The night I cried myself to sleep. My first love was a short-lived one, as are most friendships in the military.

Best Buddies

I met my first lover when I was three years old. He was five. Of course, back then I had no idea what would be happening fifteen years later.

It all started on the night of my eighteenth birthday. We were out raising hell somewhere and were just a little tired. We decided it was time to go home. As we pulled into my driveway, Mike put his arm around my shoulder, and we started to talk. That wasn't unusual — he did it all the time, even in school. He was just a very physical guy.

He talked about how long we had known each other and how we'd grown to be very close friends. "People say it's almost like we're married because we're together all the time," he told me. And it was true.

But then he really surprised me. He said, "I wish we could be more than just best friends." Now, you have to remember, I was only eighteen and still a virgin. The clues he was giving me went by completely unnoticed.

About two weeks later things came to a head — so to speak. As we sat in his mother's car, in the garage, we began to talk. We went through the usual bullshit of the day, and then the conversation turned to us again. But this time it was different. Instead of putting his arm around my shoulder like he usually did, he put his hand on my knee. I wondered about it but said

35

nothing. As we talked, his hand slowly moved up my leg. This started to worry me a little.

The next thing I knew, his hand was on my crotch. The conversation was still very vague, and his hand didn't move — it was just there. Silence fell upon us. Suddenly my fly was open, and he was bending over my crotch.

When I asked him to stop, he just told me to relax. I didn't think I'd ever be able to relax again.

Before I knew what was happening, I felt a very hot sensation on my dick. This was something very new to me, and I didn't know how to react, so I just sat there. Then it started to feel pretty good — better than I had thought it would. From someplace deep inside me came a noise like the purring of a lion cub — animalistic and sexy. This seemed to spur Mike on all the more. I remember the feeling of his cute white nose on my crotch and the feeling of my seven-inch black dick down his throat. After I came — and I mean right after — Mike got up and walked out of the garage. I went home.

The next morning I went to his house, as usual, and found him sleeping. I slowly and very gently put my hand on the bulging basket in his Jockey shorts. It felt very warm and soft. I couldn't believe how much it felt like my own.

Mike stirred a little but didn't wake up. I slowly rubbed his cock the way he'd done mine the night before. I felt his dick starting to get hard. I tried to work up the nerve to put it in my mouth, but I just couldn't. It was then that I heard him moan. Mike was waking up, and I was getting scared. I took the chair at the foot of his bed and waited for him to open his eyes. When he finally did, he quickly covered himself with the blanket.

He asked me if I'd thought about what had happened the night before, and we talked about it some. It didn't take long for us to figure out that we wanted to do it again, so Mike got up and locked his bedroom door.

By the time he walked over to me, I was so hard, it hurt. But he didn't open my pants and start feeding on me this time.

Instead, he mouthed my cock through my sweatpants. He took off my shirt and licked my nipples — first the left and then the right. Nobody had ever done that to me before; it felt terrific.

When he finally moved back down to my cock, I thought I would come just from feeling his breath on its head. First he played with the ridge, smoothing his tongue over the edge and into the slit. Then he dived onto the shaft, swirling his tongue around and deep-throating my entire seven inches. Up until this time I had pretty much let him do what he wanted, but I could no longer keep my hands to myself.

I grabbed at him, scratching his back and almost drawing blood. I reached down and started to jerk him off. He couldn't stop me from moving all over the bed. I had a grip on his dick that must have been painful for him, but I couldn't help myself. I came harder than the night before. My cock head was sensitive when I was finished coming, but he kept sucking me — almost to the point of pain.

Mike, still on his knees, began to jerk himself off. His hand moved with lightning speed on his organ. As he leaned back on his heels, I moved to the floor. Reaching out, I grabbed his dick and hesitantly brought it to my lips. My breath fell heavily on the head, and my tongue slowly moved out to touch it. When it finally did, I was really surprised at its taste. I tried to do all of the things that Mike had done to me, but I couldn't keep up. After gagging a few times, I realized that my deep-throating needed work. I was rewarded sooner than I had expected, with a sudden burst of come from Mike's dick.

We lay there awhile, panting, trying to collect ourselves. It was then that he turned over and kissed me — a French kiss, at that. He got up to shower, and I walked out into his backyard. For the rest of the day, neither one of us said a word.

Balancing His Beam

was sitting in a wide straddle position on the mat, stretching and warming up for the gymnastics meet. Even though I'd been in gyms all my life and rubbed shoulders and patted rock-hard butts with my teammates, I still couldn't help getting turned on every time I entered the gym and spied those outstandingly compact bodies.

This time, though, there was nobody else there to attract my attention — or the attention of my horny cock. I had gone earlier than the rest because I usually took longer to do my stretching routine.

Actually, it was fortunate that I was alone because I had a hard-on. As I bent over the mat and stretched my muscles to the limit, I realized that I had been unconsciously grinding my cock into the floor and pumping, as if I were humping the floor.

I had just started to get into it when a rival of mine walked by, close enough for me to get an eyeful of the mass encapsulated in the expanding crotch of his nylon shorts. I had to look away to compose myself.

He casually walked past me and toward the horse, where he passed the time by chalking his hands and peering slyly over his shoulder at me.

I folded my legs, feeling my muscles relaxing, and then stood up. My hard-on wasn't subsiding, so I bent over and placed my hands flat on the floor to stretch my hamstrings (and to hide my full boner).

My ass was raised high in the air, and I was peeking between my legs when I noticed the hunk strolling back across the floor, headed right past me, toward the parallel bars. He came right by me again, stepping between the cables and my ass — a very tight space of only a foot or so. Then, just when he was directly behind me, I felt his basket lodging itself squarely where my ass and legs came together.

Before he disengaged, he thrust his pelvis forward and mashed his cock and balls into my legs and ass. Then, in a voice that would melt Siberia, he said, "Hey, sorry, man."

He glanced quickly around the gym and saw that nobody else had arrived yet. Turning his intense blue eyes toward me, he said, "I need some tape, and I don't know where the training room is. Do you?" My cock kicked in my shorts.

"Yeah," I replied, "I'll show you."

We went up the stairs at the back of the gym and made our way to the training room. I took him around the back way to another smaller room — the one the contestants usually kept their gear in. I walked in ahead of him and heard him close and lock the door behind us. When I turned around, he was rubbing the incredible bulge in his shorts.

"Here, let me make that more comfortable," I said. "Your jock seems to be a little confining." I went over and released his almost-erect cock. It was already bigger than anything I'd had in the past year.

I took his cock in my mouth and licked around the whole shaft, slicking it up and readying it for deeper penetration. I swirled my tongue around his meat, which was as hard as his washboard stomach. "Hey, can you do me a favor?" I asked. "I've always wanted to deep-throat a guy's dick while he was doing a handstand!"

"Sure," he grinned. He then kicked up into a full handstand, and I grabbed his ankles and put my mouth over his big meat. I

39

pushed the head past the back of my throat and jammed my face hard into his groin. While I was going up and down on his shaft, I grasped his ass cheeks and dug my fingers into his flesh.

I released his cock and moved over to the mat, lying on my back and inviting him to lie on top of me. He joined me, pressing his rock-hard body along the length of mine. His cock head played with my asshole, steadily pushing against it. Then he pushed his cock all the way in and started fucking me, in and out, faster and faster. He was ready to come but held off, grabbing my cock and jacking it.

His come shot out in thick waves, and I felt his warmth covering the insides of my ass. Then my own thick wad shot up and splattered his perfectly defined chest and stomach muscles.

"Wow! Thanks," he said. "I don't think I need that tape anymore." We got ourselves together and headed downstairs to where the rest of the gorgeous men were already swinging, straddling, flipping, and checking out everyone else.

Dirty Laundry

I think that leaving New York is the best thing I could have ever done. And Los Angeles seems like it's just what I need. My new condo, which overlooks Griffith Park, is just fantastic. I can scope out all the nearly nude male sunbathers below without being too obvious. Sometimes I watch them and jerk off at the same time. Judging from the action I spied from my bedroom window in just the first weekend, I could tell right away that I was going to like it here.

I got a job right away too. But I didn't have to start it for another two weeks. That was great because it gave me a chance to explore my neighborhood — and my neighbors. The pool downstairs looked like a real cruisy area; just checking out the prime meat gathered around it made my dick hard. I especially liked the pretty blond in the Speedo. Man, was he hot! I was anxious to get my face up against his pretty ass, but I was much too shy to approach him.

One day, though, I cruised down to the laundry room to wash the clothes I'd dirtied on my cross-country drive, when lo and behold, who should I see putting his jockstraps and other goodies into the spin cycle but my favorite blond.

I watched him sorting through his clothes and putting them in the washer. Dropping his seventy-five cents into the slot, he walked past me without saying a word — he didn't even nod.

jack hart

After he left, I quickly opened his washer and started rifling through his clothes; I just had to know more about him. Most were soaking-wet, but I managed to find a pair of Jockey shorts that weren't even damp.

Delicately I removed them from the washer and lifted them to my face, savoring the fragrance. Swooning from the smell of his sweaty come, I held on to his shorts with one hand and rubbed my crotch with the other.

Now, I know I said I was shy, and I really am — with people. But with some guy's briefs, I'm right at home.

I was just about to put them back and sneak up to my apartment for a quick jack-off session when I heard a voice behind me: "See anything you like?"

I spun around and found the blond staring at me, a smirk gracing his beautiful face. I panicked. Ashamed of myself and hot for his body, I stammered and let my arms fall limply, trying to cover my erection with my hands.

He walked closer and looked me in the eye. "You like these so much?" he said as he took them from my hand. I dumbly nodded yes.

"Well," he continued, "how'd you like to see me in them?" He cocked his head to one side and smiled. "Twenty minutes — your place." Then he was gone, leaving me shaking and trembling in the laundry room.

I ran to my apartment and checked it out, making sure it was at least presentable. After a few minutes I heard a loud knock at my door.

When I opened it, the blond was standing there, wearing nothing but the Jockeys I'd admired earlier. I thought I would shoot my load as soon as I saw him. The briefs were well-worn, especially in the crotch. I dropped to my knees immediately and pushed my face into his basket, inhaling his sweaty odor. I could feel his cock harden.

I pushed my face deeper into his crotch and gave his cock a playful bite — I could tell it was a whopper. I slowly slipped his underwear down, revealing a beautiful blond bush, into which I slowly buried my face. I took the head of his cock into my mouth, feeling my own precome oozing from my now–rock-hard dick. I licked and sucked his massive boner, which was also wet with precome. I grabbed his balls, but he turned around quickly, grabbed his ass cheeks, spread them apart, and ordered with a gasp, "Eat my asshole!"

I was never one to refuse a good ass, especially one as hairy as his — it had delightful blond fuzz all over it. I pushed my face in, got a good whiff of man odor, and then dug in, chewing and biting on his juicy ass meat. He spread his cheeks farther apart for me as I licked and sucked.

He moaned as I chewed on his man hole, sucking up all the juice his furry butt hole could muster. He got down on all fours and spread his hole. I took this as an invitation and dived down farther into his crack.

Then I raised up a little and took my aching piece in my hand, spitting on the shaft and slicking it up for easy entry. Holding it by the base, I eased the fat head into his hole till it popped. He moaned again, and I grabbed his hips and jammed my dick in to the hilt, leaving him thrashing about on the floor beneath me.

When I heard him mutter something about the pain, I shoved even harder — just my way of letting him know he'd have to take it like a man. I slapped his ass as I rammed into him, feeling his ass juices flowing. I fucked him hard and long, with wet, juicy strokes, then I pulled out almost all the way and heard a little sigh of relief. With a mischievous grin, I slammed back in, causing my cock to explode inside his ass.

He shuddered, and his body shook as he collapsed on the floor beneath me. I hovered over him, dripping with sweat and tingling all over. My tired arms could no longer support even my own slight body weight, and I slumped down on top of his sticky, sweaty back.

Gingerly I nibbled at his neck and kissed his earlobes, trying to get my energy back up. As I lay there, exhausted and com-

jack hart

pletely spent, all I could think of was how much I was gonna love it here in my new home.

Dining Out

Some of the best sex takes place in the men's room. Along with those who come in to relieve themselves, adjust a tie, or wash their hands, there are those who come in to wait. They wait to make contact and eventually have some of the hottest, hardest sex known to man.

The thing they find most attractive about public sex is the unknown: Is he married, a student, or someone who came in just to jack off but decided to stay and enjoy the warmth of another man's mouth? *Hell,* he tells himself, *it's not like I sought it out, and who's gonna know, anyway?*

Yet once he's tasted the fruit of forbidden sex, chances are he'll return the next time he gets horny, giving less and less thought to anything other than the gut-wrenching climax that's available just for the asking.

Of course, I didn't know any of this prior to visiting this one particular rest room one lunch hour. I spotted a pair of tennis shoes crouched against a wall, and I heard the sound of intense fucking going on. It was so strange, especially because all the other guys in the head acted like they didn't hear a thing.

For the rest of the day I found myself thinking about that scene in the john. Later that evening something drew me back. I loitered, reading the graffiti on the walls and examining the discreet holes in the walls separating the toilets. I started to feel

45

pretty stupid, remembering how many times I'd studied those hot written messages, failing to realize they were serious business — there were others as horny as I was.

I didn't have too long to think about it, though. Footsteps, the squeak of an adjoining door, and a great-looking pair of hairy calves caught my attention. I watched, transfixed, as they slowly strode into the next stall. I crouched and peered through the hole in the wall: A tall, well-built blond was standing only inches from my face.

I drooled as he pulled his tight white T-shirt up over his muscular chest, revealing gorgeous pink nipples. His strong hands lazily — almost absentmindedly — pulled on his dong.

That beautiful uncut cock appeared to be close to nine inches in length. It was so thick, I was sure it would tear my lips if I ever got the chance to suck him. The head darkened to a purplish pink, and thick, corded veins stood out along the surface of the shaft. His wang arched and throbbed with each stroke of his fat fingers, and a clear ooze dripped from the slit.

This got me hotter than I'd ever been before. My aching prick made a decision for me. *Take a chance,* it said.

I passed a hastily scribbled note under the partition: "I need to have your cock shoved so far down my throat that you spray your steamy load and make me swallow all the come. I'll give your balls a good licking until your cock is hard and throbbing. You can blow all your jizz in me."

I watched as he unfolded and read it. He hesitated. I started to sweat when he pulled a pen from his pocket and wrote a response. Tearing the paper from his fingers, I read: "I'm pretty damn horny. I'll probably blow your head off. What the hell, though, let's go for it."

He dropped to his knees and inched under the partition wall.

Just then, however, the door to the head creaked open. I sat completely motionless as my friend scooted back over to his stall. Silently I cursed the bastard who was taking so long to piss and wash his hands.

After what seemed an eternity, he left. My neighbor fell back on his knees and moved closer toward my grasp. Stroking the hairs on his crotch, I bent to take the head of his cock into my mouth. I could hear him sigh as he inched forward and drove his erection deep into my mouth, finally stopping as my nose came to rest in his wiry pubes.

I pulled him farther under the wall and moved my mouth up and down his hard prick. Quicker and quicker, harder and deeper, he worked it in and out of my mouth until I felt him stiffen.

"Oh, baby," he moaned loudly. "Suck that hard old dick." Then he dumped a wad in my mouth. It eased down the back of my throat and into my hungry belly. I felt him relax as he pulled out, and I kissed the head of his softening rod, cleaned the come off his shaft, and rubbed my face on his hairy thigh.

I'd never had sex like that before — fast and urgent. The possibility of someone's coming in had made it only hotter.

Moments later I heard him leave. When I opened the door, I found a new message written on the wall. DAILY SPECIAL: EIGHT-INCH TUBE STEAK, SERVED IN A NEST OF BLOND HAIR, WITH TWO HARD NUTS. CREAM IS EXTRA.

Ring of Fire

I ached from the extra strenuous workout I had just put myself through. As I pulled off my wet tank top and tossed it into my locker, my muscles bunched from the movement. *At least the hard work is paying off,* I thought. My shoulders, arms, and pecs had at least doubled in size. I admired the results, flexing, looking at myself in the mirror. Too bad nobody was there to enjoy it with me. I sighed and ran my hands over the mounds of muscle on my chest. My overly sensitive large brown nipples hardened in response to my touch and the cool air in the locker room. I could feel my cock start to respond too, lengthening and filling with blood.

At that moment the door to the locker room swung open, revealing four guys I recognized from their frequent group workouts. They were not my kind of men, though. All I had ever heard them talk about was bars and tricks.

I grabbed my towel and headed for the showers, trying to conceal my burgeoning erection. The water was already running when I got there, so I braced myself for the fluctuating temperatures caused by the club's antiquated plumbing system. Stepping under the hot waterfall, I soaped up my body slowly, paying attention to my still-hard nipples and my dick. I had often fantasized about meeting a guy who was really into my nipples. I had met men who had played *at* my tits but never *with*

48

them. I wanted more than just licking and pinching; I wanted twisting and biting till my tits hurt.

Since I didn't want to pop a load in the shower that day, I rinsed myself off and stepped from the shower. The first thing I noticed was that my towel was gone. The second thing I noticed was that it was already in use, drying off one of the most perfect bodies in my gym. I had often admired this blond from across the Universal machine or the dumbbell racks, but I had never seen him like this. He was totally naked, his sun-bronzed skin showing no tan line whatsoever, his muscles accented by the water he had not yet removed. He looked like he'd been lifting weights since he was ten. His curly blond hair clung to his wet shoulders and fell loosely over his forehead. As I looked up into his eyes (he had to be six foot three or so), I was amazed at their color. They looked like the blue you see in Navajo jewelry, turquoise. He grinned at me shyly.

"Oops — guess you caught me," he confessed. "I was hoping to be dry and out of here before you finished. I forgot mine," he added, sheepishly handing me the towel.

I was dumbstruck. "That's okay, I guess, no harm done," I finally managed to sputter. I was blatantly staring at his chest the entire time. He had the best set of pecs I had ever seen — two big slabs of carved beef, capped by nipples that looked like caramel kisses, wrapped in the silkiest-smooth skin I'd ever had the pleasure to gaze upon. But the really amazing thing about his tits was that each was pierced with a thick gold ring! I had always fantasized about piercing my tits but had never had the courage to do it. I just had to meet this man.

"Well, see ya," he said good-naturedly, turning and heading for the lockers.

This was an opportunity I was not going to miss. I followed him to the locker room, toweling myself with the already damp piece of cloth as I went. I spotted him at a locker, pulling on white boxer shorts. I had been so fascinated with his tits that I hadn't even checked out his cock. Hell, I didn't even know if he had one! Well, if his dick matched the rest of his body, I knew I didn't have anything to worry about.

"Do you always use other people's towels when you forget yours?" I asked with a grin, approaching his locker. "Not that I mind," I quickly added, bringing the towel to my neck.

"No, yours was the first," he chuckled. "I really apologize."

"It's okay," I said. "Actually, it's the first time in my life I ever wished I could be a towel myself."

He looked startled at first. *Uh-oh,* I thought, *maybe that was a mistake.* Then he laughed again.

Feeling emboldened, I asked him my next question. "I hope you don't think I'm getting too personal, but I was just wondering, um… I don't know how to ask this really… I was looking at your tit rings." *And not just those,* I thought to myself.

"Oh, yeah. A friend did them for me," he replied. "You really like them, huh?" He swelled his chest up, proudly displaying the heavy gold circles.

Do I ever! I thought. "They look really great," was all I could think to say.

"You should get some if you like them so much," he offered. "You've got great pecs," he growled, roughly grabbing my left tit. "Lots of meat on 'em."

This is going to be easier than I imagined, I said to myself. "How about going for a drink?" I suggested. "I know a great place not far from here."

"I don't drink," he said tersely. "How about we skip the preliminaries and go to my place instead?" he asked, his blue eyes twinkling. "I'll let you look at 'em real close-up."

In no time at all we had reached his apartment. As soon as we walked in the front door, he was stripping the T-shirt from his magnificent upper body. "I don't like to wear clothes at home," he explained. "I'm sort of a nudist."

"Hey, whatever," I replied. "It's your house." Again I found that my eyes were drawn magnetically to those pierced nipples. They looked so hot!

"Man, you really get off on these don't you?" he asked again.

"Yeah, I guess I do. I always had this fantasy that someday I could do it. But I just never found anyone who could do it — or just never had the courage," I admitted.

"If you really want it, anything is possible," he said, "anything at all."

He crossed the living room floor, dropping his yellow nylon shorts as he approached me. "Why don't you let me help you out of those clothes, and we'll see what else you would like?" he asked, grinning at me.

In no time I was naked beside him. He leaned down to kiss me for the first time, his tongue tasting salty-sweet. I released his mouth, dropping to my knees slowly. Soon I was facing one of the most beautiful cocks I had ever seen. It sprang fully hard from his gold pubic hair, thick at the base, with a slight curve toward his body, tapering to a juicy peach-colored uncut head. The foreskin was retracted only about halfway off the head when I tongued it back, uncovering the tender skin beneath. I plunged it into my mouth, licking and sucking for all I was worth. I withdrew almost all the way, licking again around the sensitive head, then toyed with the foreskin by pulling it all the way forward and then back again. I licked the entire shaft from head to base, dropping my tongue to taste his low-hanging balls. The taste of his precome was salty-sweet, just like his mouth. He moaned softly, my head between his big hands. I played with my own dick as I pinched my nipples with my other hand. I could tell from the way his huge balls were drawing up that he was getting close.

Just before we got to the point where there would be no turning back, he pulled me off my knees. His cock was still hard and twitching, dripping saliva and precome. He kissed me again, our tongues wrestling forcefully. He pulled away and looked at me. "Let's go to the bathroom," he ordered.

Puzzled, I obeyed. *Well, maybe he likes it in the bathroom,* I thought, *and at this point, who cares?*

jack hart

Dropping the lid on the toilet, he sat down on it, his prick still hard and waving in the air.

"Come on over here, baby," he cooed. "I'm going to make you feel really good."

As I walked over to him he opened a condom package and unrolled it over his swollen member.

"Take some of this and rub it on my hot dick," he commanded, handing me a tube of lubricant. As I leaned over to carry out his order, he inserted a slick finger into my asshole, working it around and making me twice as hot as before.

"Sit on it, baby, facing me," he whispered, grabbing the base of his mammoth piece of meat.

I slowly lowered myself onto it till that point when you just have to have it all or you think you can't stand it. When it was all the way inside me, I started moving the muscles of my ass around it, giving him a good massage. My ass was filled to the max with his hard dick. Then it happened. He pinched my nipples hard. I thought I was going to pass out. Then, when the pinching started to feel good, he added a twisting motion. My tits responded by getting hard as rocks and pointing to the skies. Soon he was twisting them like he had lost his favorite radio station. Meanwhile, I rode his dick up and down, sliding onto it with ease. Every once in a while I would stop at the low point to grind it a little. He especially liked that, I could tell.

I was in heaven, and from the noises he was making, so was he. Just as I felt myself getting close to shooting, he stopped again. He held me down all the way on his prick.

"Slow now, slow now, baby, let's make this last," he purred. "There's something else I have for you. It's a surprise."

What he was doing felt fine to me. He reached up into his medicine chest and withdrew a small bottle, a paper packet, and something else I couldn't see. I started to get the feeling I knew what was in store for me.

With his dick still hard inside my ass, he used a little piece of cotton and some alcohol from the small bottle to sterilize his hands and my left tit. He opened the paper packet and removed a needle.

"This is going to hurt a little," he said. "If it hurts too much, just grab on to me."

No problem, I thought. What an unbelievable night! He was using his thumb and forefinger to make my tit harder still to ease the needle's entry. Slowly he inserted the thin piece of steel through the sensitive flesh. When the needle went through, I must have flexed my ass muscles because he jerked his cock in my ass as if in response. Before I knew it, the needle was out, and a gold circle had replaced the hole it left in my left tit.

I wanted to give myself over to him completely. "Now, finish what you started, stud," I growled.

He picked me up just like that, my legs around his waist, and carried me into the bedroom, positioning me on my back on his bed. After he got me there, he began to pummel my now-dripping ass cheeks with his hard meat. I reached around, grabbing his hard butt and pulling him into me. He began to pull on my neglected dick and coaxed it into readiness once again. As he bent over me, I grabbed his earlobe with my teeth and then licked and sucked his neck.

Soon my cock was convulsing, sending globs of hot white come into the air, arcing over my head. At the same moment, he came in my ass for what seemed like an eternity, again and again flexing his dick muscle inside me. He collapsed on top of my now–come-slicked chest, breathing deeply.

I looked down at my newly acquired tit ring, admiring it.

"Looks hot, doesn't it?" he mumbled.

"Oh, yeah," I agreed. "Just tell me one thing."

"Anything."

"When you're ready to do the other one, will you let me know?" I asked, leaning over to kiss him.

jack hart

Cycle Sluts

An avid bicyclist, I try to ride several centuries in Northern California each season. These are not only a great workout, with lots of new scenery, but they are also a chance to ride with several hundred young athletic men wearing nothing but skintight spandex shorts and jerseys.

In late summer of 1989 I was riding a century out of Santa Cruz with an especially good-looking group of riders. The morning passed uneventfully as I spun through cool coastal redwood forests, checking out all the men. By midafternoon we were well inland, it was hot, and the pack of riders had thinned out considerably.

I had been gaining on a solo rider for some time, and as we took on a long, gradual hill, I was content to keep my distance some fifteen yards behind him. Short ringlets of black hair stuck out from under his helmet. Since he was wearing nothing but black cycling shorts detailed with red and white thunderbolts, I could study his physique in detail.

He had a classic cyclist's build. His triangular torso was trim but well-developed, giving him lots of strength for long climbs such as this. He had a small waist, and his buns were perfectly round, firm, and tight. His legs were lean, straight, and powerful. The fact that they were shaved gave him away as a serious cyclist.

54

HEAT

Just watching him in motion, his legs spinning, ass firmly planted on the saddle, was making my testicles tingle. Although the hill we were climbing was long, hot, and treeless, I knew from the prior year that a side road ahead led to several shady and secluded rest spots. I decided to make my move.

As I pulled alongside him, I shouted, "Hey there, I'm Rex. Nice shorts."

It was only then that I realized what a prime USDA-choice hunk I had on my hands. The rest of him was as tight and trim as his ass. He wore Oakley reflectorized sunglasses. His face was angular, tanned, and rugged, with a black mustache to match his curly hair. His cycling gloves didn't hide powerful hands, long fingers, and perfectly manicured fingernails.

"Thanks," he replied, flashing me a smile that made my heart take two extra beats. "I saw you coming up behind me and thought you'd pass me by now."

"Oh, I've just been enjoying watching you," I said.

Little did he know that the head of my cock was saturated with precome as a result of watching him ride.

We talked bike talk for several minutes, about chain-ring sizes, derailleurs, and brakes. He described in detail the kind of lubricant he used on his chain. All I could think about was what kind of lube I wanted to use on him.

We were fast approaching the side road. I mustered all my nerve and said, "This is getting to be too much like work. I know a place ahead where we can take a breather."

"Sounds great. Lead me to it," came his reply.

With a burst of energy, we both charged ahead, turning off the main road into a quiet grove of trees. We leaned our bikes against a tree and fell, panting and laughing, in a heap on the grass. We were both propped up on our elbows, facing each other. Minutes of silence passed as we gulped cool slugs of water from our squeeze bottles.

In those minutes I watched a small bead of sweat trickle slowly down his temple and leave a moist trail along his neck. Then

55

it cascaded over his shoulder, gaining speed down his chest as it passed his firm button-shaped nipple. Merging with other beads of sweat on his slightly hairy chest, it formed a rivulet through the curly black hair just above the top of his shorts, terminating in the damp mustiness below.

I realized that simply watching him had left me with a huge hard-on, because my cock was surging inside my tight shorts, straining to stretch out to its full length.

Because of his sunglasses, I couldn't see his eyes, but it was becoming clear to me what he was looking at. With a slowly pulsing rhythm, his dick grew and grew along the inside of his right leg till the glistening, throbbing head emerged from the leg of his shorts.

He took off his sunglasses, revealing intense steel-gray eyes that twinkled with excitement. "I've got to get these shorts off before I strangulate myself," he said, as in one clean motion he pulled them completely off. Without a word, I followed suit.

The sight of him would have invigorated the most exhausted athlete — tall, tan, and sculpted, he looked like a marble statue come to life. I moved over to him, touching his lips ever so gently with mine. His response, though gentle also, included a brush past my lips with his tongue. I took the plunge. We intensely explored each other's lips, teeth, and tongues. After long minutes of French kissing, he pushed himself away slightly; his tongue traced a path across my chest, circled my right nipple several times, then traveled slowly down through my chest hair to just above my prick.

He paused a second and then suddenly took my whole shaft, all the way up to my balls, into his mouth. The sensation sent a shiver up my spine and caused me to scream out in pleasure. Obviously enjoying himself, he worked my cock up and down till a white froth appeared around the corners of his mouth.

By this time we were on top of each other, licking, kissing, moaning, and sucking each other fast and furiously. With every thrust I felt the blood pulse in the tip of my cock, sending waves of pleasure to my brain. His cock was a thick, straining mass in my mouth, and I could tell from his stream of precome and his thrusting ass that he was as close to climax as I. After half a dozen more searing seconds, we both screamed in ecstasy as we shot long, creamy streams of come all over each other and collapsed together in a wet, sweaty, come-soaked mass.

Putting his arm around me, he said with a laugh, "I thought we were going to take a breather. I'm glad we didn't. By the way, my name's Brad."

Realizing that the sun was beginning to set and that we still had a long way to go to the ride's finish, Brad and I reluctantly pulled on our shorts and set off again.

UPS Delivers!

Living alone in an old farmhouse in rural North Carolina, my nearest neighbors a mile away, I often get lonely and start daydreaming about gay encounters. But one day I had an encounter that was better than any of my dreams. It all happened because I had ordered some gay videos. They were shipped UPS.

I had just stepped out of the shower, had a towel wrapped around my waist, and was drying myself off. Then there was a knock at the back door. (Everyone comes to the back door of this old farmhouse.) When I answered the knock, there was this hunk from UPS dressed in a brown uniform. His muscles were so huge that they stretched the brown cloth to the limit across his upper torso. He had a small waist. His lower torso and basket were disguised by the bagginess of the jumpsuit. Reading from the address label, he said, "Don, it seems I have some videos for you. I need for you to sign for them." He added a sly grin and stared at the bulge of my crotch through the towel.

While I was signing my name, he asked if he could use the bathroom, adding, "Man, I gotta go. My name's Sam."

He didn't close the bathroom door behind him. He asked if I ordered a lot of videos. Then he unzipped the jumpsuit all the way down to his crotch and started peeling it off. I got a look at his hairy chest. Sam pulled the jumpsuit down to his ankles as

58

he sat on the commode to piss. I walked into the bathroom and resumed drying my hair with a hair dryer, but I angled the medicine-chest mirror so I could also watch this hunk.

He looked up at my reflection, then ran his hand down between his thighs. When he had finished pissing, he pulled his cock up and shook it several times, slapping it against his belly. Though still soft, it was long — at least nine inches and rather slender with a gorgeous cut head. Under the towel, my uncut dick started swelling. The UPS man leaned back on the john and started jacking off, slowly rubbing that long cock of his.

I turned to face him. His shaft turned into a flagpole and was poking into his navel. Glistening drops of precome shone on the glans, which he grasped lightly as he jacked himself. Simultaneously he rubbed his chest, stopping to tweak his tits. The excitement I felt made me gasp, which caused my towel to come loose and fall to the floor. My cock was sticking straight out, right at Sam's eye level.

"Man, an uncut cock — my favorite kind," he said, wasting no time in grabbing my eight-incher and massaging my ample foreskin between his thumb and forefinger. Then, just as suddenly, he pulled back the hood to reveal my throbbing cock head. Slowly he tantalized that sensitive head as he licked up and down my shaft, but at last he popped me into his warm, juicy mouth. Sam's tongue threaded its way under the foreskin. His cock-sucking experience showed as he quickly brought me to climax, deep-throating my dick and swallowing all my jism. It had been so long since I had been with another man that I shuddered convulsively when I came.

"Well, I gotta be goin'," Sam said as he reached down to pull up his jumpsuit, but I grabbed him by the waist and pulled his backside toward me. With my left hand I massaged his furry chest and hard tits while pumping his stiff cock with my right hand. Soon I realized that I needed the fingers of both hands to encircle that big, long dick if I was going to do it justice. In the mirror I saw his big balls draw up into a tight knot. It didn't take long for Sam to shoot his load into the john. Turning him around to face me, I licked his cock clean.

He left soon after that, saying he still had a lot of deliveries to make and reminding me always to specify UPS delivery.

Excuse me, but there's a knock on my door.

Batting Practice

I joined the company softball team for two reasons. First, it was a good way to stay in shape. I have a great body, but I have to work hard to keep it that way. Second, softball seemed a great way to meet sexy guys. And believe me, there were plenty of them out there on the field.

Ironically, none of the players attracted me as much as the coach did. Hank, in his early forties, worked out every day, so he had no hint of middle-age bulge. He was lean and muscular, and he moved with a panther's supple grace. When he hit the ball, the muscles of his upper back and shoulders rippled; when he ran the bases, the muscles in his thighs stood out.

Hank had black hair (the kind that shows highlights of blue), gray eyes, and a wide mouth.

I didn't realize he'd noticed me until last week, when he asked if I'd like to stay after practice. "Maybe I can help you with your swing," he said.

I wiped my sweaty forehead with my bandanna and said, "Well, I could sure use the practice. I guess I could stay a little longer..."

"Oh, come on," Hank joked. "You can't be that tired out."

I wrinkled my nose. "You don't think so?" I said. "Then you try standing out in right field for a few hours with the sun beating down right on your head."

Hank looked at me with mock ferocity. "I have," he said. "I used to play semipro. Or didn't I tell you?"

By now I could tell that he was as attracted to me as I was to him. His eyes were sparkling, and his gaze was traveling up and down my tight T-shirt and cutoff jeans.

"So, we going to practice later, or what?" he asked.

I was feeling a little reckless. "I'll stay if we can rest a bit first," I said. "Right now I need some water."

I walked over to the team's cooler and poured some icy water down my parched throat. It tasted so clear and good that I wanted to feel some on my body too. I decided to tease Hank and began dripping the cold water along my arms, all over my face, and down my chest. Hank just stood there, staring. His shorts were bulging as I walked back to him.

I picked up my bat, hitting it in the dust a few times — like I'd seen other players do. "I'm ready!" I called.

Hank answered jokingly, "Play ball!"

After practice it didn't take long for the other players to disappear. Hank and I were left alone on the field. It was time for our special session.

Hank stood behind me. He encircled me with his arms, his biceps gleaming with sweat, to show the correct batting posture.

He held me close. I could feel his heart beating against my back and his cock swelling into the crack of my ass. I wiggled my backside against his immense shaft and was rewarded by feeling it twitch in response.

Hank nuzzled my ear. "Shall we go into the dugout?" he asked, his voice urgent.

My throat had become too dry to answer, so I just nodded and followed him.

He unbuttoned my shirt and pushed it down my shoulders, admiring my chest. The cool breeze drifted over my nipples. But that isn't what made them stiff and rigid; it was Hank's gifted fingers. He grazed them gently. Then he took my left nipple into his mouth and nibbled on it before moving on to the right.

Before I knew it, I was naked, facedown on the bench, one leg over each side of it, and Hank was fondling my ass.

I sighed as he caressed me. There was something very arousing about being exposed to him like that.

I could hear him slipping on a condom. With strong hands Hank lifted my hips slightly. Then I felt each inch of his velvet shaft as Hank yanked me to him, filling my ass with his meat. I yelped and whimpered as his love pole stretched me, pummeled me, filled me deliciously.

I rested my cheek against the vinyl of the bench, eyes closed, groaning loudly.

He turned me over and lifted my legs. Eagerly I flung them over his shoulders. Hank leaned forward. He placed the head of his cock back at the entrance of my waiting ass.

"Oh, yes," I said, smiling broadly.

Inch by inch his hot, smooth cock disappeared into my ass, once again deep within me. As he rammed his rod home, Hank bit my lips and kissed my throat.

His strength was overpowering. My knees, high in the air, bounced with every powerful thrust of his pelvis.

As I climaxed, the walls of my ass gripped Hank's love handle. Then he too exploded; I felt his prick jerk and spurt inside the condom.

Hank kissed me hard and held me tight. "That was great," he whispered, breathing into my ear.

My fingers rubbed against his back, and I kissed his lower lip. "I think I'm going to need lots of coaching, don't you?"

Ever since then Hank has made me put in a lot of extra practice sessions. And I can't say no to the coach.

Doing Time

As I walked toward the recreation yard to start my daily workout, I felt something strange in the pit of my stomach. I had been in the joint for eleven years — that's 4,015 days to someone on the inside. And if prison teaches you anything, it's that life just grinds on and on, day in and day out, with a mind-numbing sameness. That's why it made me so uneasy when I woke up and felt, well, different for some reason. I didn't know why; I couldn't put my finger on it.

As I lay on the incline bench and began my reps, I heard my buddy Eric behind me: "Hey, Mikey. Tough load you got there."

I turned my head to see Eric standing directly over me, grinning, as I struggled to set the bar back up in the brace. "Yeah," I said. "It is. Feel like getting some? We could spot each other."

Eric grinned again, his eyes lingering for a moment on my muscular torso. As he considered my offer, my eyes were drawn to his crotch. Not that I was checking him out or anything, but the way we were positioned, with his straddling my face, I couldn't help noticing that he wasn't wearing a jockstrap. His cock and balls were clearly visible as I looked up through the legs of his workout shorts. I had a great view, and I wished that he would just take a seat — right on my face.

"Sure," Eric said, snapping me out of my fantasy. "Let's pump some iron, dude."

64

As I looked up at his hairless and tanned muscular frame, my balls began to stir with excitement. I felt my cock beginning to strain against my jockstrap, and I don't think any of this escaped Eric's eyes.

We had a great workout; we always did when we spotted one another. We liked each other a lot and spent a lot of time together; of course, time was all you could spend in the joint. Neither of us would openly admit it, but we'd lusted after one another for years. We had our macho images to protect, however, and would never have risked a moment of intimacy.

As we walked back to the cell block, Eric told me his cell mate had just been released and that he'd like me to transfer in. I didn't want to seem too eager, but I told him, "Sure."

The next day we got an okay from the warden, and soon I was packing up and moving to Eric's cell. As I went to take a shower the first morning, my nuts were on fire; I couldn't imagine how two studs like Eric and me could share a cell without some heavy, hot, sizzling sex.

I was definitely hot for him. He was a great-looking stud. He was half Spanish and had the sparkling looks of a Latin stallion. It was obvious that even at the tender age of twenty-four, he had spent many years building up his body. His arms, chest, stomach, and thighs were rock hard and beautiful. He had an ass that made my cock swell every time I looked at it. And he was hung like a bull. Once I got the pleasure of seeing him in a jockstrap; his stud meat completely filled the pouch. No doubt he packed a heavy gun and a big load.

At 10 o'clock, right on the button, our cell door slammed shut and locked. I had gotten settled into the top bunk. Eric and I had had fun all day, talking and joking around, but when those doors shut, the atmosphere felt different immediately. The heat we were generating was overpowering.

We had both stripped down to our shorts and were lying in our bunks, making small talk. Then, when I least expected it, he said, "Say, Mike. How big is your cock?"

I was floored. I couldn't believe that he had come right out and asked that.

As my heart pounded against my chest, I tried to think of a cool response.

"Why do you ask, Eric?" *Great,* I moaned to myself. *Real cool move, jerkoff.*

"Because I've been checking you out, and you look like you got a big dick there. Besides, I heard you got at least nine and a half inches."

"What?"

"Yeah. Check these out, man." Eric stood up from his bunk and tossed me a magazine. I almost shit; it was the same fuck magazine I subscribed to. No big deal, right? Well, it was a *gay* fuck magazine, and I had a personal ad in that very issue!

I suddenly noticed that all Eric was wearing was a worn jock-strap. His dick was clearly swollen inside that pouch, and his fat balls were hanging out the sides. His bushy pubes stuck out too, making the jock look at least two sizes too small. I tried to pretend I didn't notice.

"It's a fuck book, bro," Eric said. "With some pretty nice-looking studs. Hey, check out the classifieds."

I was nailed. Eric had known all along, and now he was leaning back against the wall with a cocky smile on his face, totally enjoying my discomfort.

I calmly turned to the classifieds and found my ad immediately. Eric was by now gently rubbing his stud cock, making the head stick out of the waistband. He wanted action, and I knew there was no way around it.

I looked at my ad and saw that Eric had circled it, adding a handwritten message in the margin: "Let's get naked and freak, big boy."

I lay back on the bunk, contemplating my next move. This was incredible, and the excitement of being found out by Eric had me hot. By the time he spoke again, I had decided to give it all to him.

"Listen," he said finally. "I dig you, and I've been wanting that hot body of yours for a long time."

"Really?"

"Yeah, check it out." Still leaning against the wall, he now had a playful look on his face. One of his hands was moving over his chest, and he'd stop now and then to pinch his hardened nipples. His eyes were locked on mine. Eric was massaging the enormous head of his cock with his other hand.

"Wanna see the rest of it?" he asked.

Before I could answer, Eric eased the jockstrap down to his thighs and waited for my reaction. He knew he was making me hot, and he made it worse by playing with his nice, big nut sac and stroking the entire length of his shaft for me. It was at least eight and a half inches of thick cock.

Without a word I pulled back my sheet. My dick was hard and straining to get out of my shorts, which I quickly removed. Eric watched me, still slowly pumping on that fine meat of his. As I lay back, staring at Eric, I slowly jerked my own dick, feeling it grow larger and larger as Eric's eyes remained frozen on it. I knew he couldn't believe my size and perhaps was now wondering if he could handle me.

"Jesus, I knew you were *big*, but..."

"I'm just what you need, Eric," I said. "Besides, who started this anyway?"

I jumped off my bunk and went over to our cell door. I reached up and turned out the lights and stood with my back to Eric, looking out the door and listening for any guards who might be in the area. The mounting excitement was incredible. The possibility of being caught by the guards or of being overheard by some other con made it all the more exciting.

Suddenly Eric came up behind me. I froze, still standing against the bars, looking out. He began to rub and massage my ass, running his fingers gently up and down the crack.

He slowly stepped in closer, wrapping his muscular arms around my waist and pushing his crotch tightly against my firm butt. He slipped his cock between my bare ass cheeks and began humping his dick against my ass, allowing his rod to glide up and down the crack of my warm ass.

"God, you're great," he moaned, working his hands over my chest, pinching and pulling my hard nipples.

I responded by reaching back with one hand and grabbing his muscular ass cheek, pulling him in close to me, and fingering his very hot butt hole.

"I wanna fuck," Eric moaned softly in my ear and then kissed and nibbled the back of my neck and shoulders.

Without a word I reached back between us and placed his cock against my asshole, feeling it slide in deep. I exploded in pain and pleasure as Eric's thick stud meat worked its way in and out of my tight, virgin ass.

He placed his hands on my hips and began pumping his meat into me faster and harder, almost lifting me off my feet with each thrust.

I now had my hands wrapped around the bars, holding on tight and meeting Eric's thrusts with my own, wanting every inch of his dick in me. It was great. I felt like an animal in heat.

In between thrusts, Eric could not resist taking his hand off my hip to stroke my steel-hard cock and squeeze my balls.

Eric was now fucking me like a madman, trembling and shaking, kissing and biting my back. I was sure the guys in the next cell could hear our panting and moaning, but I no longer cared. I was in love with this hot man who was boning me so passionately. All I cared about was giving him all the pleasure he could possibly stand.

I felt the hot burst of Eric's load exploding deep inside my body, and I tightened my asshole like a vise around his cock, milking it of every drop of protein. As he came to a stop, Eric left his cock in me for a final moment's pleasure, playing and pulling on my dick, getting ready to service what now belonged to him. I could feel the sweat on our bodies mingling and inhaled the glorious aroma of two studs in heat.

"What a fuck you are! God, you are good," Eric said as he went to his knees and licked my asshole clean.

"Yeah? Then how about taking care of this?" I asked, turning around to face him.

Eric grabbed my giant tool with both hands and began stroking it as he kissed and licked my thighs, slowly working his way up to my swollen balls. "Jesus, Mike," he gasped. "I can't believe how big you are!"

He then proceeded to give me the best damn blow job I'd ever had. As Eric kissed, licked, sucked, and admired my fuck stick, I knew that I'd be with this stud for a long time to come and that this was only the beginning.

Copy Cock

recently purchased a home, a real fixer-upper. As a result I was making regular trips to the local hardware store, and over time I became acquainted with a stud employee there. John was always a lot of help. He's my age — thirty — and stands six foot three, with tanned, rippling muscles. Every time I looked into his blue eyes, I got a raging hard-on. And though I wasn't certain, I thought I detected similar interest on his part. I began going to the hardware store more and more often, making up problems, buying items I didn't need, all the while plotting ways to bed this hunk.

Finally I got the nerve to invite him over to see what I'd done to the house. I could barely contain my excitement by the time he arrived, but I offered to show him around. I conveniently ended the tour in the master bedroom, and after a few awkward moments I made my move. I told him I wanted to reward him for all his help. He stepped forward and put his arms around my waist. Jackpot!

In just a matter of moments, I had him stripped of his clothes, and before me stood an absolute god. His chest was huge, his stomach flat, and his only body hair was a small trimmed patch above an amazing appendage that was easily eleven inches long when hard (which it was). In a flash I was mounting his battering ram, which stretched my asshole to its limit. He threw me on my back, and I grabbed my ankles and spread wide for the pounding of a lifetime. His length and girth caused sensations never before felt in fucking, and soon, without even touching my own rock-hard dick, I shot a huge load. Moments later he pulled out and shot his massive load to the farthest corner of my bedroom.

The next day I went over to his place, hoping for some more action. As we talked I noticed a paper bag bearing the name of his hardware store sitting on the coffee table. He reached into the bag and removed a container of artist's molding plaster and two tubes of white silicone. "What's this for?" I asked.

John explained how he'd watched with envy as I enjoyed his massive dick up my ass, and he asked me if I would help him with a project. I agreed and followed his instructions, which were to open his pants and take his shaft into my mouth. In no time I was gagging on his full length. At his behest I then tied a leather strap around the base of his cock, swelling it to even greater proportions. John mixed the plaster while I covered his shaft with lube. Together we covered his massive dick and balls with the plaster, then we waited for the mixture to dry.

The plaster was set within ten minutes, and I tugged it gingerly off of John. Out slid his cock, leaving a perfect mold of his dick! John then filled the mold with silicone. An hour later we broke the mold, and an exact duplicate of his cock was formed, veins and all!

John wanted desperately to be fucked with this newly made clone of himself. I loosened him up by plugging him with my fat seven inches, which he seemed to enjoy, and then my fingers — one, two, three, and ultimately four. Finally, I inserted the massive silicone monster. John gasped as the tip entered his tight hole, but gradually he relaxed, and I worked it all the way in. I began fucking him with it, slowly at first. He moaned with pleasure as I slid the dildo in and out, in and out, slowly building up speed and pressure. "Faster!" he screamed. "Harder!" His balls pulled close to his body, and, without touching his cock, he came, shooting huge bursts of white cream all over his chest and face. The show had me so hot that I quickly followed suit.

John and I had great sex for the next few weeks, but then he stopped calling. I suspect that since he got his copy cock, he doesn't need me anymore.

Close Shave

J eff owns a barbershop at the west end of a local strip mall where all of the stores share a common sidewalk and a long green metal awning. His shop is unidentifiable except for an old-fashioned barber pole with a red-and-white swirl that spins around in circles and lights up after dark. Jeff keeps his barbershop open late in the evenings, which is fortunate for confirmed night owls like me.

One night I spotted the lighted barber pole from the road and decided to stop in for a much-needed trim. Jeff greeted me with his customary smile as he swiped a straight-edge razor up and down a worn leather strap that was hooked to the back of his chair. Jeff is around thirty years old, I guess, and extremely well-built, and he has a handsome, clean-shaven face. He keeps his hair clipped fairly short, but his meaty forearms are covered with a mass of hair. This evening he was wearing a pale short-sleeved shirt, and a comb and a pair of scissors were jutting out of the breast pocket. Lots of crisp, dark hairs were visible at the open neck of his shirt, which told me he was probably pretty hairy all over.

"Here, have a seat," he said, motioning me into the red leather barber chair.

"Thanks," I said as I settled back into the comfortable old cushions. "Much obliged."

jack hart

With a bit of a flourish, Jeff draped an apron over me and fastened it around my neck. "So what can I do for you this evening?" he asked.

"Oh, I think just a trim tonight will take care of it," I answered, thinking at the same time how I wouldn't mind receiving a lot more attention from the sexy barber.

Jeff went right to work with his scissors and comb, slowly circling the chair as he meticulously snipped at my hair. When he hovered at my right side, it seemed as though he was pressing his cock into my arm, but he kept his eyes glued to my head. As he stepped back to assess his progress, I brushed his dick with my fingertips, making sure to keep my touch light enough that it wouldn't arouse his suspicion and would seem, if anything, like an accident. But I left my hand in place on the armrest, open and with the palm turned upward.

"Mmm, yeah," he said, keeping his eyes on my head. "I like that." Then he very deliberately pressed his cock into the palm of my hand and slowly rocked back and forth. I clutched his hardening bulge through his trousers, and as I did so I slid my other hand down to my crotch to stroke my own stiffening dick in rhythm with his gyrations.

"Here, let me help you with that," Jeff said. He flung the apron off me and pulled my pants and underwear down around my ankles. As soon as my cock sprang free, he sank to his knees in front of me and wrapped his lips around it. He took the entire length of it down his throat and bobbed his head up and down my tingling shaft.

He sucked me till I was on the verge of shooting. I wanted to prolong the pleasure, so I cupped his face in my hands and pulled him up. "How about if you shave my balls?" I whispered into his ear, and he quickly agreed.

My pubic hair was fairly long, having not been trimmed in a long time, so Jeff started out by cutting most of it off with a pair of scissors. Then he stood and went to the counter, where he filled his hand with menthol shaving cream from a heated dispenser. When he lathered up my balls, I winced a little from the sting. He spread the lather around with a soft-bristled brush, and the sensation suddenly began to change from burning pain to cooling pleasure. I spread my legs to accommodate the blade of his straight razor, and he shaved me clean with short, swift strokes, stopping now and then to rinse the razor in a bowl of hot water. The heat of the razor and feel of his hands as he stretched my balls to keep them smooth made my dick stand up in a quivering state of excitement. Every few seconds or so, he would wrap his free hand around my cock and give my shaft a couple of strokes. I was so close to the edge from all this attention that my dick was oozing a constant stream of precome.

Jeff finished shaving me and then followed with a vigorous rubdown with a warm, moist terry cloth towel. Then he wrapped the towel around my cock and stroked it till I sprayed those big hairy forearms of his with a huge load of my very own brand of shaving cream.

Night Depository

I work in a small branch of a bank, and close by is a retirement center. Most of the employees come into our bank to cash their paychecks. One particular young man, Rick — Mexican, light-skinned, muscular build, in his early twenties — comes in often to make deposits or inquiries. He wears his work clothes, light tan shorts and a button-down shirt with the company emblem. The shorts are skintight and don't leave much room for anything in the pockets.

One day Rick came into the bank and approached my station. He said he needed to make a deposit. I couldn't help noticing that he had an erection, which was showing very plainly through his tight pants — it appeared to be a good seven inches in length and at least six in circumference. Well, this caused quite a stir in my slacks. I was tempted to reach over and latch on to this marvel, but I somehow resisted. Rick finished his business for the day and left, leaving me with a squirming cock that needed to be satisfied. I proceeded with my normal business, however, and finally forgot about him.

Several days later Rick came in again, and I'll be damned if his cock wasn't hard again. He came up to me and wanted to get the balance on his account. Well, I just couldn't hold back any longer, so I leaned over toward him. I looked him straight in the eyes and said, "Rick, if you ever come into the bank again with your manhood showing like that, I'll reach over the counter and check out your assets." He didn't say a word or even pull back; he just looked into my eyes and smiled. He got the information he needed and was on his way.

It was almost a month later when he came in again. I was in the office alone, as my partner and I take turns going home early on Fridays. Rick walked up to me and looked around the bank, noticing that no one else was there. I couldn't help seeing that his cock was a good eight inches hard. I looked around, reached out, and placed my hand where his cock was showing through his pants. He just smiled. I looked at the clock. It was 6 p.m., so I walked over to the front door and pulled it closed, flipped the lock, then walked back to Rick. I started toward the back — where the break room was — and said, "Come with me." He did, with no hesitation. Once in the break room, I reached out and put my arms around his waist, pulled him close to me, and gave him a big hug.

I ran my hands underneath his shirt and up his muscular chest, slowly rubbing it and pinching his nipples. Rick pressed his cock tightly against me and forced his tongue deep into my throat. I ran my hand down his chest to his rippled stomach, found a patch of hair around his belly button, and gently ran my fingers through that. Then I undid the snap of his pants, unzipped his zipper, and pulled them down. As his pants cleared his pubic area, I looked down to discover that he wasn't wearing any underwear. His mammoth eight-inch cock sprang up toward me. I pulled his pants down to his ankles and dropped to my knees. Rick chuckled and said, "I've come to make a deposit," then placed his hands on my head and pulled it toward his towering cock. As he pushed his dick against my lips, I opened my mouth and ran my tongue across his piss slit, licking the sweet, salty ooze. He started to quiver a little, so I took the entire swollen thing into my mouth and started to suck. Rick pushed himself closer to me, forcing the remainder of his dick clear to the back of my throat.

jack hart

I ran my hands up the backs of his legs as he pumped steadily into my mouth. Rick kept this up for about ten minutes before I felt his ass tighten up and the head of his cock get bigger. Sliding my fingers down between his two luscious buns, I pulled them apart, exposing a hairy bung hole. Rick arched his back, his cock pulsing, and I could feel his hot come hit the back of my throat. After about five big jets, Rick pulled me to my feet. "That was great!" he said.

By this time my cock was standing at full attention. Rick reached down, felt my crotch, noticed the large bulge, and swiftly undid my pants. He took hold of my six-plus inches and started to jerk me off. He moved around behind me, still massaging my cock, and I felt the massive head of his dick nudging my ass. He pressed firmly with his cock against my bung hole and pulled me back with such force that his cock penetrated my hole with ease. "I have one more deposit to make," he said, "and then you can close."

Before I knew it he was all the way into my ass and pumping for all he was worth. I nearly climbed the wall each time he drove his eight inches into me. The head was rubbing against my prostate, and I knew I would blow shortly whether he kept jerking me or not. *Whammo!* My first two wads hit the top of the vault. And before very long, Rick managed to blow another load. He then pulled out, wiped his cock off, pulled up his pants, and smiled at me. I pulled up my pants, and we walked back out to the lobby. He started for the door, turned to me, and said, "Thanks for taking my deposit so late. I'll be back one of these nights to make a withdrawal."

David's Big Bulge

My first sexual experience with another guy remains my all-time favorite. I worked my way through high school at a hometown grocery store. It was a good job, and I was good at it, so by the time I was nineteen, I was often put in charge on quiet days and weekends. I was popular with the customers and knew most of them. The one important person to this story is a guy named David, who was in the store often, either shopping for his mother or just hanging around.

I teased David a lot. He was very small, and his size made him an easy target, but he knew the teasing meant that I liked him. He went along with all of it, coming back with a fast answer when I made a smart remark and putting up a good fight when I wrestled with him. He was really a cute guy — blond hair with blue eyes, slender as well as short, and a bright smile that made it impossible not to notice and like him.

One Sunday, when I was working with just one other checker in the store, David came in to get some things for his mom. He didn't appear to be in any hurry, so I suggested he come along with me and talk while I worked in the back room. We started to joke around as we always did, and when David told me it was his eighteenth birthday, I told him I wanted to be the first to give him eighteen pops on his ass to commemorate another year of growing up.

jack hart

David dodged as I reached for him, but he wasn't quite fast enough. I grabbed him and picked him up, turning him upside down. As I let him down, I still had hold of the waistband of the shorts he was wearing. When he tried to pull away, the zipper of the shorts tore open. I hadn't meant to do that, and I was really sorry about it. I told David to take them off and let me try to fix the zipper.

We went over to a corner of the back room, behind some boxes, and he pulled off his shorts. I tried to fix the zipper, fiddling around with it for a couple of minutes before looking up at David to tell him it was no use. He was standing there watching me, wearing nothing but his briefs, and it was obvious that he had a hard-on. The size of it was something else, especially on such a little kid! Those shorts bulged out like there was a softball inside them!

"Looks like you have a problem," I said teasingly.

For once, David did not have a sharp comeback. He blushed and smiled, then said, "Yeah, I guess so."

By that time I had a hard-on too, though I didn't tell David. Sex hadn't been on my mind when I'd suggested he take off his shorts. I'd never done anything in my life with another guy, but seeing that big bulge in David's shorts really turned me on. I guess I knew at once what I wanted to do, though I didn't know exactly how to accomplish it. But that didn't keep me from trying. I asked David if he had that "problem" often, and he said yes. "What do you usually do about it?" I asked.

"Well," he started, "if I'm alone, I play around with it."

"Why don't you do it now?" I said. "I don't mind. I might even like to watch."

"Well, maybe," he said at last, "but only if you do it too." I guess that's what I wanted him to say, though I told myself I'd just watch without getting involved.

He reached over and pressed his hand on my jeans over my cock. "Looks like you've got just as big a problem as I have. Let me take it out for you."

80

He started to unbutton my jeans, but I told him, "You first."

He stepped back without argument and dropped his shorts to the floor, baring it all for my viewing. A fat circumcised dick popped out, complemented by a sac of nuts indeed as big as a softball. It looked even more huge because David was so small. I couldn't take my eyes off it, and I wanted to touch it, though I was still a little afraid.

David wasn't. He got his hands back on my jeans, and this time I let him open them up and pull down my shorts. As he grabbed hold of my dick, I couldn't ignore the urge to reach over and touch his crank, then begin to squeeze and jack it gently. It felt good to have his dick in my hand — but not better than having him pump my cock. That it was happening in secret, in the back of the store, added to the adventure.

I didn't have long to think about anything, though. David suddenly said to me, "If you promise not to get mad, I'll show you something else we do sometimes." Getting mad was the last thing I was likely to do, and I told him so. At that he knelt down in front of me and took my cock into his mouth! What a feeling that was! I had heard about getting a blow job but had never experienced it and hadn't begun to realize how wonderful it could feel. My breath was taken away by the strength of the sensations as David's wet, warm mouth consumed, groomed, massaged, and loved my dick.

At first he took only a little more than the head into his mouth, moving back and forth on it. But after a few minutes he went all the way down on me, somehow getting my whole piece of hard meat into his tiny mouth. The feeling was absolutely fantastic! The only trouble was that it didn't go on long enough. It seemed no time at all before David stood up again and, grinning, told me, "Now you do it to me."

That took me by surprise. I hesitated for a second, but the excitement of the moment drove through my inhibitions and powered me onto my knees before the abundance of sexy equipment staring me in the face. I took it into my mouth. Oh, my

jack hart

God! The feel, the taste, the warmth, the fullness, the muscularity; it was exciting as hell! Although I wasn't as good at sucking as David, I know I got really charged up doing it.

The more I did it, the more I liked the feeling of that big dick working its changes in my sensitive mouth. Responding to the massaging of my tongue and lips, it stiffened, jerked, throbbed, and put out a variety of tastes, temperatures, and textures for my exploration and stimulation. The more I did it, the more I liked feeling that fresh manliness. David finally pulled me off and said, "Better stop. I'm getting close to shooting off." I'd been jacking myself off while I sucked him, so I was near the mark too. "Let's just jack each other off now," David said, so we grabbed each other's dick. Almost immediately David's let fly, shooting a mess of sticky come all over my hand. He started working furiously on mine, and in seconds I went off too. David kept his hand moving on me until he had pumped me dry. We painted our hands and cocks and balls and asses and abs with hormone-laden man sauce.

As we wiped ourselves up with a handkerchief, he looked up at me and said, "If you want to come over to my house tonight, we can do this some more. My mom goes to work at 8 o'clock, and I'll be there alone."

"Okay," I promised.

He pulled on the shorts he'd been wearing, telling me with a grin that he'd have to hold the bag of groceries over the open zipper all the way home. I felt guilty and remembered a safety pin I'd seen by the cash register, so I made a quick trip and found it. As I pinned David's shorts, his teen dick got ready to play again, moving about and pushing against my hand. He gave me one last grin and waved as he sailed out the door, holding the bag of groceries in front of him.

I couldn't keep what had happened off my mind all afternoon. I must have looked at the clock every five minutes, wishing time away till closing time. I reached home, ate dinner, showered, and changed clothes. I told my folks that I was going to see "a

82

friend," then had to walk around the neighborhood for about half an hour so I wouldn't get to David's place too soon.

I timed it just right, he told me as he opened the door. He had on a different pair of shorts, bulging at the crotch with a telltale hard-on hidden inside. I had one too. He led me upstairs to his room and closed the door behind us. Wasting no time, we both got naked.

We just lay there for a while, each playing with the other's dick. "You want to try something else that's fun?" he asked me.

"I guess," I said, "but this is fun already."

"Yeah," he said, "but you could fuck me in the butt if you want to."

He reached over to his dresser and grabbed a jar of Vaseline and a towel that were lying there. Telling me to stand up, he took some of the Vaseline and smeared it on my dick. Then he lay down on his back, lifting his legs and feet high toward my shoulders, telling me to get between them. I stepped into position, got my knees on his bed, and pointed my hard-on at his hole. "Take it kind of slow at first," David instructed, reaching a hand down to guide my dick to the right spot. For a moment I wondered how it would ever fit in the ass of such a little guy, but I needn't have worried. I felt the head suddenly pop through the ass opening, and I stopped. David breathed in quick, shallow bursts. I didn't move. Then he said, "Okay, slowly, a little more," and I went ahead, meeting resistance at a second tight spot. I pushed real easy and could feel myself entering the gate as it slowly opened and David relaxed.

I thrilled at the sensation of his warm ass. He said, "You can fuck me hard now," so I took him at his word and drove every inch of my dick deep into him. He lifted his ass to meet my movements each time, and the feeling got better and better.

I don't think I could have stopped even if I'd wanted to. Moving back and forth faster than ever, I drove my dick deep into him over and over, then suddenly found myself in the grip of a mighty orgasm. I lunged forward to bury my shooting cock

jack hart

deep in my friend's ass and lost my entire load in David's innards. I watched him tighten his face muscles, open his mouth, force his eyes closed, stick his tongue out, grasp my cock with his already tight asshole, and suddenly spring off a walloping load of cream that left long white streaks all over his chest.

With each spurt his ass squeezed desperately on my spent cock, causing it to suddenly spring back to life. Miraculously, I felt on the edge again, and my now totally stiff dick expanded within David's ass and caused both of us to grind into an extended orgasmic feeling that lasted and lasted before each of us had a great dry nut bust together. I collapsed onto David's warm sweat-wet body with my own, and we lay there entwined, embracing. We both fell into a deep sleep.

A few hours later David's mother called to say she wouldn't be home. David would be alone all night. "Want to stay?" he asked. "I'd be happy to have a bed partner." I called my folks, telling them my friend would be alone, and they okayed my staying over.

We alternately slept and played throughout the night. I'd had a wonderful time and promised him as I left that I'd join him the next evening after work.

As I showered and got ready for work the next day, I had to take a short break to jack off, recalling the feeling of David's big bulge — his swollen dick in my hand, mouth, and ass! It was the beginning of many new and exciting times with David.

Easy Street

One evening this past fall, as I sat looking out my window, I saw my next-door neighbor returning home from work. This man is my idea of perfection. I had harbored this opinion for about a year but never made any overt advances because he is very straight-appearing.

After he entered his house (and my raging fantasies subsided), I returned to removing my clothes from the dryer. I started folding laundry and began once again to dream of the hunk next door. I'm not sure how much time had passed, but I was roused from my reverie by a knock at my door.

I had not been expecting anyone at this time of day, and I was clad in only a pair of red bikini briefs, all my other clothes having been in the wash. I went to the door and peered through the peephole to see my next-door neighbor standing there. Since I wasn't completely naked, I opened the door slightly and poked my head out to see what he wanted. He informed me that his phone was out and that he would like to use mine to report the problem to the phone company.

I opened the door wide and invited him in, and as he entered, I noticed his scanning my body from head to toe, his eyes lingering for an extended period about midway between. I became very anxious, acutely aware of my near nudity. I felt the stirrings of an erection as my cock, barely concealed by my scant briefs

jack hart

to begin with, began to poke its way out. *My God!* I thought. *He'll think I'm a pervert!*

I stammered something lame about doing housework and quickly directed him to the phone. After what seemed like hours, he turned and walked to the phone, muttering something about how he usually does housework in the nude and how I had no reason to feel embarrassed about my state of dress.

While using the phone, he kept his gaze decidedly fixed on the bulge in my red briefs. By this time the head of my cock was poking out over the top of the waistband. He hung up the phone after a few minutes, and I decided to offer him a cup of coffee, which he accepted. As I poured the brew, I could feel his gaze on me. I felt somewhat uncomfortable but excited, and my cock was rock hard with anticipation.

"You're in pretty good shape," he commented.

"Thanks," I replied, my voice cracking in my throat. I suddenly noticed that his running shorts had become quite distended in the front.

He took a sip of his coffee and put the cup down. "Do you have any sugar?" he asked.

"Yeah, sure," I replied and walked into the kitchen. I was reaching up to the cabinet to get the sugar when I felt his strong, hairy arms encircling my waist. He had followed me into the kitchen and was now standing directly behind me, his cock rubbing up against my ass.

"I've waited a long time to do this," he whispered in my ear. His voice was like velvet, making me shiver with passion.

I turned and kissed him, slipping my tongue in his mouth and attempting to devour him right then and there. We stood there kissing and fondling each other for a while until I reached down and removed his running shorts. I was delighted to find a beautifully shaped seven-inch cock surrounded by a thick bush of glistening black pubic hair.

I pulled away and led him into the bedroom, where we fell side by side onto the bed. We kissed some more, and I began to massage his adorable ass, exploring his crack and placing my index finger on his pucker. He moaned and raised his left leg to allow me better access.

After a few more minutes of this, I rolled him over on his stomach and reached into my night table for a condom. He took it from me and began opening the foil package. I almost shot my load as he unrolled it over my cock. Condom in place, I proceeded to rim his warm pucker. He writhed and moaned underneath me, raising his ass up off the bed.

This was all the prompting I needed. I moved up on his back, placing my cock head at the entrance to his asshole, pushing gently. He pushed back into me, letting my cock enter slowly. We lay quietly for a while so that he could get accustomed to the invasion of my massive cock in his virgin asshole. Soon I began pumping in and out of him slowly, feeding his ass more and more of my meat. He matched me thrust for thrust, his sweaty buns bumping up against my pelvis. I began to fuck him furiously, slamming into him for all I was worth.

He cried out after a few more thrusts, and I felt his whole body shudder as he came. This pushed me over the edge. I felt spasms rock my entire body as I filled the condom deep in his ass with my hot come. We were drenched in sweat and breathing heavily, as though all the oxygen had suddenly been drained from the room.

We lay there kissing for a while afterward, caressing each other's bodies. We agreed it was the best sex we'd ever had. I guess sometimes you don't have to look too hard to find the right man — he may be right next door!

Attention, Shoppers!

I work as a sales associate at one of the nation's largest retail chains. Our store is open twenty-four hours a day, and I work the night shift. After midnight the crowds disappear, and the store grows so quiet that you could hear a pin drop were it not for the carpeted floor. Which reminds me, on the night I first encountered Fred, I was on my hands and knees picking shirt pins out of the carpet. He appeared from around a corner and asked, "Do you have any colored underwear? You know, like those fancy bikini briefs?"

He stood about six foot two and had a lean physique, with dark brown hair and a clean-shaven face. He wore stonewashed jeans and a brown leather jacket, unzipped. He didn't have a shirt on underneath, and I could see a finely etched chest covered with a dense mat of hair and capped with a pair of pert nipples the color of café au lait. His chest hair gave way to a thinner trickle of hair down the center of his torso. It wrapped around his navel, spreading out into the shape of a triangle that peeked out above the waistband of his jeans.

I led him to the underwear aisle and pointed to the racks of bikini briefs. He picked up a red pair that had been torn out of its package. He gently fingered it. He didn't seem the least bit embarrassed or uncomfortable with himself. "Do you mind if I try these on?" he asked.

I took him to the fitting room, unlocked the door, and stepped inside. Fred stepped inside too and locked the door behind us. He unbuttoned his fly, hooked his thumbs in his side belt loops, and pulled his jeans down around his ankles. He wasn't wearing any underwear to begin with!

I dropped to my knees and eyed his package up close. His cock sprang up straight out in front of me, fat and stiff — a full eight and a half inches. His ball sac was big and bulging like an overripe Georgia peach, covered with fuzz and bursting at the seam down the middle.

I took his cock in my hand and tugged it back and forth. His ball sac swayed with each stroke. Next I wrapped my lips around the bulbous head. He leaned back and withdrew it momentarily, only to shove it back into my open mouth. He rocked his hips and continued to thrust, ramming his rod all the way down my throat. I reached up and ran my hands over his hairy belly and chest. Then I reached behind him and clutched his ass cheeks. Suddenly his whole body tensed. He shuddered, gasped, and spewed forth a heavy load of hot come, which I devoured. I sucked every last drop until his dick was soft.

Fred bought the underwear and came back for more the following night. He's spread the word, and some of his friends and acquaintances have come in for my personalized customer service. Now I sell more underwear after midnight than most salesmen do all day!

Pubic Transport

I don't usually kiss and tell, but this is one story I just can't keep inside any longer. It happened about a year ago when I was working for a bank on the other side of town from where I live. I didn't have a car back then, so I took the bus to work every day. It was about a 45-minute ride each way — which wasn't so bad, actually, because it gave me a chance to read the morning paper and relax a bit before my hectic workday and to unwind on the way home.

The bus route I took was not a particularly crowded one — mostly senior citizens on their way to see their doctors or winos camped out in the back of the bus, snoring away. Often it seemed that I was the only person riding this bus who had a job! Hardly ever did someone sit next to me; there were plenty of empty seats, and I usually liked to spread out my paper, discouraging anyone from thinking about taking the seat adjacent to mine.

At any rate, one day on my way to work the bus stopped in front of an apartment complex, picking up one passenger. I wouldn't have noticed him at all had he not sat down next to me on the aisle. I remained fixed defiantly in my window seat, burying my nose in my newspaper, trying to block him out of my peripheral vision. *For Christ's sake,* I remember thinking, *there are plenty of empty seats. Why does this asshole have to crowd*

90

me like this? He had ruined my morning, as far as I was concerned, and I resented him for it. Until I looked at him.

I stole a sidelong glance at him as I put down one section of my paper and picked up another. I saw the most beautiful green eyes staring back at me, framed in a gorgeous face set in a shock of blond hair. Like me, he was wearing a business suit, which framed his broad chest and shoulders nicely. He was absolutely devastating. Flustered, I quickly turned back to my paper. When I looked again a minute later, he was staring straight ahead, seemingly oblivious to my attention. *Oh, well,* I said to myself, *guess I scared another one off.* I turned back to my paper, trying to put him and his amazing-looking body and face out of my horny mind.

It was then that I felt a hand move across my left thigh and toward my crotch. I froze. *Jesus,* I remember thinking, *what the fuck's he doing? Doesn't he see that there are other people on the bus?* Using his right hand, he deftly managed to undo my belt and quickly unzipped my fly, reaching into my Jockeys and palming my already-stiff cock.

I was so excited, I just about shot right then. But I was also nervous as hell. Granted, there weren't that many people on the bus, but surely someone would notice something like this! I glanced around, but no one seemed to be looking our way. Just to be safe, though, I lowered the newspaper a bit so that it covered our laps.

In the meantime he had grabbed hold of my engorged shaft and was slowly stroking the length of it. I swallowed hard, praying I wouldn't let out a sound to give us away. Beads of sweat began to pour down my temples, and I was breathing heavily — albeit quietly. By this time precome was oozing from my cock, and my mystery hunk was using it to lube my shaft. Soft, squishy noises started to emanate from my crotch area, which only increased the sensations and excited me even more. I looked around nervously again. I had to bite my lip to stop myself from crying out.

jack hart

A few more strokes, and I was there. I arched my back slightly and shot load after load of hot come all over his hand and my shorts. He removed his hand, wiped it with a handkerchief that he'd pulled out of his suit pocket, and rang the bell. Brakes whining, the bus came to a stop at the corner, and he exited through the back door before I could say a word. I wiped myself off with a tissue, zipped up discreetly, and sat back, staring out the window. The bus pulled away from the curb, and I watched him walk into an office building, disappearing behind the reflective glass doors.

I thought about him all day that day and for the next several days, but I never saw him again. I'd sit upright expectantly when my bus got to his stop, but he never did show up. I never even got to say a word to him or find out his name. But I guess I don't mind, really. I'll always be grateful for what he did, and now I have a little cache of jack-off fantasies to tide me over between lovers. Public transportation is definitely the way to go!

Sex in the Sun

I t was one of the hottest summers in memory. The fire danger was so high that Griffith Park was closed to through traffic — a perfect opportunity for those of us who enjoyed romping in the great outdoors.

A Sunday afternoon in late July found me hiking up the road toward a heavy cruising area. I wore blue satin shorts and old white sneakers; a blanket and a bottle of water rode in my backpack. As the road wound around the hill and upward, the city seemed pleasantly far away.

At a sharp bend in the road there was a dusty area where cars frequently pulled off to park. Above it, connecting the two sides of a small ravine, was a high wall that created a sort of dam. I knew that behind it was an old mattress placed there long ago by a hermit. It was now used by pairs of men for whatever pleasures they might concoct.

Reclining atop this wall was a brown-skinned, nearly nude man, all blond hair and muscles. He seemed to have on nothing more than a white G-string. A bottle of oil sat next to his beach towel. My sex drive shifted into high gear.

I walked to the bottom of the wall, just below him. I put my backpack down in the dust and looked up. His belly rose and fell slightly with his relaxed breathing. Twice his arm raised, and he wiped perspiration from his face. I was sweating too. I dropped my shorts atop my backpack and stood there stroking my dick to attention. It didn't need much coaxing.

A third time he held his hand aloft, shading his eyes while he looked around. He saw me. For a moment he didn't move, and then his arm dropped, and he swung his legs over the side of the wall, sitting up so he could look down at me. His hand went to his crotch, and he pulled the soft cloth aside, exposing a thick white cock lying in his lap.

"How's about coming up here?" he said in a quiet voice. He stood up, pulling off his G-string and stuffing it into his bag. He straightened up and let me look at him. His dick was a heavy, dangling prize. "You want to play?"

"If you can't tell, then I'm doing something wrong," I said, fondling my balls. "Only, how's about you coming down here?"

For a moment he glanced up the road. He licked his lips nervously, and his big dick began to lift.

"Come on, guy," I cajoled. "Bring your towel down with you. We'll do it right here in front of everybody."

His dick was now almost completely hard. He bent over, hesitated, picked up his towel. He walked along the wall, clambered down, and came right over to me.

"I can't believe I'm doing this."

"Nobody's twisting your arm," I said, staring down at his huge erection.

Before I could reach out and caress his hard pecs or his flat belly, he dropped the towel between us and fell to his knees, grabbing my legs and wolfing my stiff penis into his mouth.

I groaned, "Oh, yeah, suck on my dick!"

He was very good. His soft lips slid repeatedly up and down my dick, his tongue played with the head, his teeth nipped along the shaft. I was getting too hot too quickly. I pulled out of his mouth against the pressure of his clutching hands.

"I don't want to come yet," I said.

I knelt with him on the towel, pulling him against me, pinning our dicks together between us.

"Oh, shit," he exclaimed, grabbing back.

His palms held my ass cheeks. Our tongues did a dance. I licked down the front of him and swallowed his ramrod dick. He moaned out loud again, urging me to suck on his hot flesh. I savored it.

"This is too good, man," he panted. "Let's get back there and do everything."

I didn't argue this time. We climbed back up and over the rock wall, taking our belongings with us so as not to be apparent from the outside. We covered the old mattress with our towels and stood facing each other, our dicks screaming for attention, our eyes glowing with lust.

We spent about three hours "doing everything." Part of the time his thick penis was sliding in and out of my joyous asshole; part of the time we lay in the cool shadows embraced in passionate sixty-nine; now and then it was me slamming my aching dick into his burning-hot anus; now and again we took turns licking one another's bodies hungrily. Finally we stood boldly in the sunlight, atop the wall, holding each other tightly as we jacked off, shooting our loads in twin arcs high above the road, just as an old man came into sight around the far turn.

We sat on the ledge together, legs spread, bodies touching, our sticky cocks dangling over the edge, while the man walked toward us along the road, staring at us. As he passed us he slowed down, looking with longing over his shoulder and finally disappearing around the next bend.

We sat like that for a while and then, with many a promise to get together again sometime, we went our separate ways. I've played with a lot of men up in the park, in sunlight and shadow, but this remains my ultimate experience to date.

Bent for Leather

For a 21-year-old small-town boy like me, gay life held many mysteries. Since I was a motorcycle rider, leathermen intrigued me the most. By chance, I came across a motorcycle-run application that sounded too good to be true — 200 men and their cycles in the wilderness for a weekend of fun.

Upon arriving at the campsite, I was completely taken aback. Never in my wildest dreams had I imagined so many hot and ruggedly handsome leathermen in one place. My mind was a mixture of excitement and fear as I suddenly realized that I may have gotten in over my head. Not knowing what to expect, I mustered all my courage and put on an air of maturity — or at least as much maturity as a 21-year-old could have.

At sundown a campfire was lit, and I was drawn to the flames like a moth, somehow hoping that the fire would replenish my waning courage. When I looked across the bonfire, I saw a man who took my breath away. He stood about six foot four, and his skintight chaps showed how solidly muscled his legs were. As my eyes wandered upward, I couldn't help staring at the leather pouch that was stuffed so full, it looked as if it would explode at any moment. His upper body had the definition of a man who worked hard every day.

As he walked toward me, his dark eyes, which reflected the firelight, seemed to be reading my every thought, and my mind raced through countless sexy possibilities. Stopping less than a foot away from me, he told me his name was Phil. The sound of his deep bass voice made every nerve in my body tingle. He invited me to a cabin down the hill where he and his buddies were staying. Trying not to sound nervous, I gladly accepted.

On the way to the cabin, I explained to him that all of this was new to me and told him I was more than a little nervous. He stopped, took me in his arms, and passionately kissed me for what seemed like an eternity. When the kiss ended we began to walk again, and he told me that I didn't have to do anything I didn't want to. He would be there to make sure of that. Suddenly I realized that we wouldn't be alone in the cabin, but that didn't seem to matter — Phil would be there watching over me.

As we entered the cabin, Phil gave me a reassuring look and escorted me to the center of the room, where he proceeded to shackle my wrists and pull them over my head. Leaving me there bare-chested, wearing only my Levi's and boots, he went to talk to his friends. I had a moment to look around. I counted fourteen men. *My God,* I thought, *fourteen men! Is this a dream or a nightmare?* Suddenly there were hands all over my body. Someone was playing with my nipples while someone else was untying my boots and a third man was unbuttoning my 501s. There was so much happening at once, I couldn't concentrate. My ass was being caressed, my balls tickled, and my nipples pinched. My mind was being overloaded by my senses.

When I finally focused my eyes, I saw a man coming toward me carrying a piece of wood with three holes in it. I couldn't imagine what was in store for me until he separated it into two parts. He placed one of my balls on one side, my cock in the center, and my other ball in the remaining hole, then proceeded to latch the two pieces of wood back together. This wild sensation gave my cock new life. Standing among these leathermen, my cock rigid, I noticed a surprised look on several faces. I was searching for Phil, suddenly unsure of myself, when he whispered in my ear, "I knew you were the right man for this job."

jack hart

Suddenly I felt a vibration on the back of my neck. The sensation moved over my shoulders and down my chest. I looked down to see a back massager in Phil's hand, which he was moving up and down my entire body. Soon other hands with various electrical toys joined in the action. Vibrators were massaging my balls, my inner thighs, and my cock as well as sliding between the cheeks of my ass — not to mention the vibrators roaming over my chest and back. After several minutes of intense vibratory pleasure, my body was tingling with excitement. Just the thought of so many men touching me all at once sent shivers down my spine. A whisper of breath on my balls almost made me pass out from the intense pleasure. I saw Phil smiling up at me as he once again let his hot breath drive me to heights I had never experienced before.

The leathermen spent hours taking my body and mind on a roller-coaster ride of excitement and pleasure. After several orgasms, my torso, legs, and arms ached with the strain. I felt my arms being released. I sighed with relief as my cock and balls were set free from the pleasurable "stock block." As my vision cleared, I saw Phil and realized he was holding me in his strong arms. He carried me to his bunk in the back of the cabin and laid me on it. He gently slid behind me and wrapped his arms around me, assuring me that all was well. We cuddled together until both of us drifted off into a well-deserved slumber of complete satisfaction.

I awoke late the next afternoon to Phil's hands gently stroking my body. He lightly kissed me, smiled, and said, "You see, leather is nothing to be afraid of. Men are men no matter how they dress."

Master Plan

I don't know why my hand trembled so as I pressed the doorbell. I had answered ads before, but this one was different. I wasn't sure if I should be embarrassed, ashamed, or perhaps a little afraid. But it was something I wanted to experience. A short, slim guy myself, I looked up hopefully at the tall, well-built man in T-shirt and Levi's who answered the door.

"Hi, Dave!" he said cheerfully, extending a strong hand to me and virtually pulling me into the condo.

"Hope I'm not late," I said dryly, noting the wide leather belt about his waist.

"Not at all," he assured me, closing the door as he looked me over. Then placing his arm about my shoulder, he said, "Let's go up to my study." He pointed to the floor above. As I climbed the steps ahead of him, his fingers sought out the cleft of my ass.

"I liked your letter," he said, going to a serving table and pouring me a small drink. "You said you liked white wine."

"Yes, thank you," I murmured, admiring how nicely his buttocks moved in the seat of his Levi's.

He snapped the cap on an aluminum can. "I'm a light-beer man, myself," he said, grinning. "Got to keep myself in shape for you guys!"

We talked for only a few minutes. Then, rising from his leather chair, he unbuckled his belt and pulled it from his waist.

"You can take your shoes and pants off for me," he ordered, "but leave your briefs on."

I did as he instructed. He reached for my arm and had me lie across the stuffed arm of his chair.

"That's it," he said, spreading my legs apart and sliding my briefs to my ankles. Then, pushing his hand between my buttocks, he worked a couple of fingers into my hole.

"Still pretty tight," he mumbled, pulling his fingers out. "Well, we'll fix that right now!" Taking up his belt and folding it in half, he began to administer a few light swats to my ass, followed by three sharper strokes that I tried to dodge.

"You said you liked the feel of a good belt," he reminded me, lashing each of my thighs. "I wish I had a razor strop!"

He held me down with one of his big hands and inserted two fingers into my rectum. My hole responded shamelessly to him. "That's better," he said. "Now we've established who's master here, haven't we?"

"Yes, sir!" I agreed as he took me by the arm and pulled me to my feet again.

"You said you wanted to experience this for the first time," he said, tossing down a small towel. "I want you to lie on your back on the floor for your master."

When I had done so, I watched with great apprehension as he removed his boots and stood above me, straddling me, facing my feet. Slowly he lowered his body onto my chest, pinning my arms under his knees while he carefully settled the seat of his pants over my face.

"That okay, Dave?" he asked. "Feel okay?"

"Yef, fir!" I answered, my nose and mouth buried in the warm cloth of the seat of his Levi's.

He sat quietly on my face while he fingered my cock and balls, then slowly rose to his knees while he unbuttoned and removed his jeans. Sliding down his dirty briefs, he lowered his bare buttocks over my face. Spreading his cheeks, he fit my nose and mouth into the crack of his ass.

100

"There you are, Dave!" he barked. "Just what you said you wanted. So enjoy!"

Repulsed at first by the strong odor of his sweaty manhood, I forced my tongue to probe the large, hairy man hole. I shot my spit-wet spear deep into his bung hole as he leaned forward and sucked my dick into his hungry mouth. Placing my hands on his wide, firm cheeks, I let myself go. This was what I had wanted. I eagerly licked the crack of his butt and contentedly sucked his ass lips.

Just as I was ready to shoot my load, he sat erect and rolled me onto my stomach. Spreading my cheeks, he slid his long, hard meat deep into my shit hole.

"Okay, little buddy," he breathed heavily, "you got what you wanted; now here comes what I want!"

He moved his hard cock back and forth inside me until I was about to come, then thrust himself into me as far as he could go.

"Ready?" he spat in my ear.

"Ready!" I gasped in anticipation.

Blast off! His stiff prick lifted me off the floor, filling my ass with thick, sticky jism, which seeped from my well-used hole and dribbled down his shaft. I shot my own load, my mouth still full of the musky taste of his ass.

Entering Freshman

I was sitting in the student union on the first day of registration, appraising the new crop of college freshmen. I saw him in line in the cafeteria. He was wearing gym shorts, an oversize T-shirt, and running shoes with no socks. His long, tan, slender legs perfectly complemented his blue-eyed baby face and the golden blond hair that fell past his shoulders to the middle of his back.

He turned in my direction, his gaze dropping straight to my crotch. I spread my legs a little to give him a better view, and his eyes rose to mine. I smiled and winked. His face turned bright red, and I thought he would drop his food tray as he started to turn away.

"No, wait," I said. "Please sit down."

He hesitated, then turned back and joined me. We made small talk while he nibbled at his lunch. When he started in on his second hot dog, I took a deep breath, crossed my fingers, and asked if he would like to go back to my room. He dropped his eyes and nodded quickly.

We walked silently back to the dorm, neither of us wanting to break the spell. When we entered my room on the top floor, he walked to the window and looked out.

"Nice view from here."

"Nice view from *here*," I said.

102

I moved behind him, put my hands on his hips, and slid them around to his flat belly, then up to his hard hairless pecs. His firm young butt pressed back against my rising cock, imprisoned in my shorts.

He turned to face me. My hands slid up his back, pulling him toward me. Our lips met, and my tongue probed deep into his mouth. He peeled his T-shirt off over his head and threw it aside as I tongue-teased one of his tiny nipples until it hardened like a pencil tip. I slid my hands under the elastic of his shorts and down over the silken skin and taut muscles of his virgin ass. His shorts fell to the ground, and he kicked them away, along with his shoes. He sat on the edge of the bed and looked up at me with a nervous grin.

I quickly stripped and sat beside him. Our lips met again as we grabbed each other's cocks and fell back on the bed. Our legs intertwined, and our bodies pressed tightly together. I stroked his rock-hard dick, feeling his quickening pulse in the vein that ran the length of it.

I knelt between his bronzed thighs and grasped the base of his eight-inch shaft with my left hand as I lightly licked the mushroom head, then engulfed it with my mouth. He groaned with pleasure as I alternately licked and sucked his enormous tool.

My right hand, cupping his heavy, pendulous balls, slid lower between his thighs, and my forefinger sought out the tight pucker of his asshole. He jumped when I touched it as if he'd been shocked.

"Relax," I said. "Everything will be fine."

I stroked his cock a few times as I gently fingered his ass, and then I turned my attention to his balls, taking each one separately into my mouth and then both at once. I raised his legs and bent them at the knees so that his puckered prize was revealed.

His asshole was perfect — pink, tight, and hairless. I almost fainted from the rich aroma that arose from the strong young man. I touched the delicate folds of his anus lightly with my tongue, and he jumped again.

103

"No!" he cried. "You shouldn't!"

I paid no attention to this outburst as I licked every inch of his alabaster buns, the tiny ridge that ran up to his balls, the deep crack. He wasn't really trying to get away; he was just a little panicky. He needed to know I really wanted him, that I knew what I was doing and that I would take care of him.

I sucked and slobbered over his twin mounds of cool flesh and clamped my lips over my ultimate objective, probing deep into his hot hole with my tongue. He moaned with pleasure, his hands scratching at the bedsheets, as I immersed myself in the heaven of his tight, young butt. Finally I pulled back and sat on my heels.

"Please don't stop," he panted, his eyes glazed over.

"Stop? I haven't even started," I whispered. I took a tube of lubricant from underneath my pillow and applied it to his opening, warming the gel first by rubbing it vigorously between my fingers.

Gently at first, then more forcefully, I probed his spit-slick sphincter with my finger, thrusting far into the hot, moist recesses of his untried man hole. I added a second digit and then a third as his muscles gradually relaxed.

"God, that feels great!" he breathed. "I can't believe it!"

"The best is yet to come," I assured him. "It may hurt at first, but just relax. I promise you'll like this."

I reached to the bedside table for a condom, opened it, and rolled it onto my swollen cock. I wrapped his legs around my neck and pressed the head of my dick against his tight rosebud. It resisted. I pressed harder, and it gave way to the bulbous tip of my throbbing prick. He cried out, a shriek of both pain and pleasure.

"It's okay," I said. "I'm going to hold still and let you get used to me. Just take it nice and easy."

I waited until his breathing slowed, then continued to press forward. My rod slid its full seven inches into his bowels. His butt gripped my tool like a tight fist. I labored to keep my strokes slow and gentle. His cries of surprise turned to greedy moans. I leaned back and pulled out.

"No! Don't stop now!" he gasped.

"Let's try something different," I said and turned him around on all fours. The sight of him like that — his long golden hair flowing over his shoulders and back, his plump white ass — made me dizzy. I moved up behind him and thrust again into his hot, hungry hole. As I pumped into him, I reached around for his dick, which jumped at my touch.

We fucked like this until he collapsed facedown on the bed with me on top of him, ramming, pounding, and thrusting until I could hold back no longer. I came, shooting jizz into his body until I thought I would never stop. Seconds later his cock erupted, spewing an ocean of come over him, the bed, and me.

We've become close friends since that momentous afternoon, but I'm more of a big brother/adviser than a steady lover. Every now and then, though, we plan a weekend just for ourselves, and we fuck each other silly.

The Right Man for the Job

I couldn't believe it. There I was, the rookie on the job site, and already I was being complimented on my fast work. I'd worked in construction once before, but that was last year, and I certainly didn't think that I'd be praised on my first day this summer. I thought my presence, at best, would be a nuisance. But the other guys seemed to like me.

I got to the site a little late, but it was okay because a shipment of air-conditioning equipment hadn't come in yet. We just sat around for a while and waited. It finally arrived at 10, and we got to work. The buyers of the condo block said they'd pay top dollar for work done ahead of schedule.

Most of the day I worked with Alfonso, a gruffly masculine middle-aged Hispanic dude with the kind of muscles you get from a lifetime of physical labor. Alfonso treated me as if I were his own kid — and not an especially intelligent one.

The rest of the crew were white except for the foreman, who was the hairiest black guy I'd ever seen. Not only did his muscles have muscles, but the hair on his chest must've been growing hair of its own. I gasped when I saw him with his shirt off.

Judging from the comments the other guys made about things like lost pieces of soap and filched underwear, I came to realize that the crew showered together in the morning before coming to work. I was about to quit right then.

106

During high school I'd had to endure jokes about the "natural man" and curious questions about my uncircumcised state. When I'd reached my senior year, my chest hair had multiplied tremendously, and my cock had grown even more than it did during puberty. The football coach said I had a "rare but welcome spurt of second growth." He thought I should be proud of my height and increased body hair. However, when examining me prior to football practice my senior year, he said he'd never seen a guy with pubic hair as thick as mine. You can understand why I felt weird and abnormal. And I definitely wasn't going into the shower with other men ready to stare and comment.

When we finished for the day, the foreman, Jerome, told me to come to the construction office in downtown Atlanta the next day before going to work. I played dumb and asked why, and he said that it was a free shower. Most of the guys went there because they couldn't afford the water bills for two showers a day. I could understand that; it would certainly save money. So I grudgingly said that I'd be there.

The next day in the shower nobody said anything, but they did stare. The reason they didn't say anything was because Jerome, Alfonso, and one of the bricklayers were uncut too. I was happy. *I'm not alone anymore,* I thought. Only two guys were as hairy as Jerome — me and a plumbing subcontractor from a small town in south Georgia.

They stared at Jerome's cock, though, which was huge and purplish black, except for the head, which was a light pink. Jerome lovingly pulled back his skin and washed the thick head. All of the guys watched, including me. It's not often that I get to see a cock as big as a porn star's. I noticed a couple of guys getting half hard, but guys did that all the time in the football showers back home, so I didn't think anything of it.

But then Jerome started getting hard. The shaft of his huge cock elongated slowly, the head getting bigger as he washed it again, slower this time. I couldn't take my eyes off his cock. He smiled at me and rubbed his fist up and down the shaft, which by now was as thick as my wrist. The tip of the thing was a rich royal purple. He milked the head again, and out came a drop of precome. I looked down at my own cock and saw that it too was getting hard.

Before I knew it, I had taken Jerome's cock in my left hand and was pulling on his stiff piece of meat. He rolled his head back and moaned deep in his throat — a gruff, growling sound that made my dick twitch. He held my prick and stroked the skin down over the head, then pulled it up and down, up and down again, until I was about to come. I wrenched myself out of his hand and grabbed him again.

I grazed my fingers lightly over his hairy ball sac and the underside of his thick root. His heavy nuts pulsed in my hand. Pulling the skin down over his knob, I pushed my thumb under the tight ridge and massaged it roughly. He shuddered as I rolled back the skin and slid my soap-slick fingers all over his dick head, which by now was the size of a tennis ball. His hairy body writhed, but I held tight to the foreskin with my thumb and index finger. His sweat mingled with the water and soap on his body and gave off a sweaty, musky man smell. He fell panting to the floor of the shower, and I unwillingly relinquished my hold on his engorged tool.

I dropped to the wet tile and scooted around until my mouth was even with his cock and his with mine. The hair on his chest scratched my stomach and tender cock head. His smooth mouth closed around my dick. I'd never felt anything so good. In return, I touched my tongue to the very tip of his foreskin-covered crown. I laved his cock with my tongue, touching areas of its head I knew would be sensitive. He cried out and wriggled on the floor like a snake. His dick grew impossibly large in my mouth. Out of the corner of my eye, I saw everyone else on our crew watching and masturbating, but I didn't care.

I started sucking in earnest, and he matched tongue stroke for tongue stroke. When I sensed that he had stopped thinking about me and started concentrating on what was happening in his own groin, I stopped for a second to remind him that there were two of us involved. When my mouth work halted, he gasped and then started sucking on me more purposefully.

I tried to match his rhythm, ignoring the feelings in the head of my cock as best I could. I reached down and fingered his huge balls. His scrotum tightened, and his meat grew even larger. He put his hands on my head and bobbed me up and down on his cock. His thick foreskin bunched up around the purple head. He arched his back, his hips pumping, and then he went rigid as his prick pulsed deep in my throat.

I realized that I was about to come too, so I clamped my lips tighter over the head of his dick and used my tongue on its sensitive upper side. His cock pulsed again, very hard this time, as his come jetted down my throat in several powerful blasts. The sweet taste of it made me shoot a fiery load of my own.

Jerome and the rest of the crew complimented me on my good work. You'd better believe I kept that job!

The Warehouseman

It was hot, and I didn't want to go to work. I knew I would have to spend the whole day unloading trucks filled with heavy machine parts. My company was moving from one warehouse to another. At least my boss had promised to give me some additional manpower to help me out.

I barely made it to work on time. But I forgot all about my boss and time card when I saw my new helper.

He was the perfect huge daddy I have always found irresistible. Big boots, big basket packed in dirty jeans, big forearms and biceps, thick chest, hairy body, and a shiny shaved head. What more could a man who wanted to be a good boy ask for? But my dad-for-a-day seemed to look right through me.

The first truck pulled up, and together we unloaded all the parts in no time. The next truck wasn't due for another thirty minutes. I guess he read my mind, because my dad wrapped his heavy, sweaty arm around my neck, then led me into an empty office in the back of the warehouse. The stink of his meaty armpit hit my nose and sent my head spinning.

Dad didn't say a word as I watched him peel off his T-shirt, revealing a magnificent chest. He grabbed the back of my head and put my mouth and tongue to use in the worship of his pecs. The fur on his chest was so thick, I worked up a sweat trying to get at his nipples. I lapped and chewed his tits until the nipples

110

were red, wet, and bigger than ever. Dad then pushed my head into his moist, musky armpits. His eager little boy laved and serviced them until they were soaked with spit, and my big daddy started moaning loudly. We were having such a good time, we almost didn't hear the next truck pull up.

We must have set a world's record unloading that truck.

As soon as it pulled away and we were back in the office, I found myself down on my hands and knees with Dad's dirty, well-worn work boots an inch from my face. They must have been a size fourteen, with at least a ten-year accumulation of dirt and scum on them. With his right boot, Dad pushed my face down onto his left boot, dragging my face across the cracked, rough leather.

My tongue stroked the soles, heels, and tops of his stinky workingman's boots. I licked up and down the laces, then up to his yellow sock tops, drinking in the smell. I was one happy son doing boot duty.

There was plenty of boot to service, but I got it all done before the truck pulled up to the dock for the third time. Dad seemed real pleased with his superclean boots, but he didn't say a word; he just grinned at me. Then he grabbed his crotch and winked. I knew that dick duty was next, and I was ready.

Primed to service some cock and balls, I was literally throwing the parts off that damn truck. Back in the office I didn't wait to be told where I belonged. I was down on my knees in a second, looking worshipfully up at the man's rough, lined face while he allowed me to feel the outline of his prick. Dad's meat grew fast and hard under his mud-caked, greasy jeans. When I didn't think I could stand to wait another second, Dad let me put my hungry fag mouth on his denim-covered cock head.

I started sucking through the jeans with all my might. I moved to the other leg and sucked the outline of his fat, full balls. I needed that cock! I wanted to feel it slide and bang in my throat; I wanted Dad's dick to fill me. I was in real need, and Dad finally let me have it. His uncut dick sprang out at me as he

111

tore open his jeans. The big man hauled out his balls, and the vapors filled my nose. I was in donkey-dicked–daddy heaven!

His construction-worker cock must have been at least ten inches long. The base seemed like it was a mile away from its fat head. I opened wide and slid the meat into my hot hole of a mouth. Dad pushed inch by inch into my head, his cock getting thicker as my mouth moved toward the hairy base. I was his, Dad's own punk, obedient son.

I pulled on his man sacs and started to chow down on the fuck pole that was quickly filling my throat. Dad held my head steady as my cock worship turned rough. I was hot for that meat pushing past my soft tongue and palate, rolling over my tonsils, pressing into the back of my soft mouth.

My mouth was stretched as far open as possible. I sucked and slurped the man dick, letting it pop out of my mouth so I could lick the huge piss slit and come-filled balls. I got my nose under his balls and sniffed up the rank sweat juice.

Four more trucks came and went. As we finished unloading each one, we would adjourn to the abandoned office. I was getting the face fucking of my young life. The more excited Dad got, the rougher he became. He held my head by my ears and went to town on me. Up and down, faster and harder, plowing in and out. The longer Dad face-fucked me, the bigger his cock seemed to get. My mouth hole was being rubbed raw. But I'm not the kind of disobedient, ungrateful son who would complain about something like that!

I brought out the rubbers when my mouth couldn't take any more use. Dad knew just how to pump my horny butt. I stuck my ass up high in the air and let that man fuck my brains out. My dad would pull it out, then — *slam!* Up my hole it went. In and out he pumped, his cock threatening to split my ass wide open. He twisted my soft nipples, yanked my balls till I squealed. He had me lying on the floor on my back, on my stomach, on my side, on all fours. The man hoisted my legs over his shoulders and crammed his cock so deep, I felt like passing out.

He set me on his lap, put his hands around my buns, and bounced me on his cock. Dad spanked my melon ass while he fucked it. The fucking went on into the wee hours of the morning. All the rubbers had been used up by the time the big guy finally fell asleep.

Not a bad day's work after all. Unfortunately, I never had another one like it, but just reliving my marathon session with Dad keeps me punching in on time.

Bus-Stop Buddies

For a couple of weeks, this new guy had been waiting at the bus stop with me. For a while we'd say only hello or talk about the weather. Larry (I found out his name) was about twenty-four, tall, and slender. He had black hair, a beard, and a smile to die for. One Friday we were talking about how glad we were that it was the weekend, and Larry asked what my plans were for the night. I said I just wanted to relax, have a few beers, and listen to music. I told him that if he wasn't doing anything, he should stop over.

Thinking about Larry later that day, I found it hard to work. I wondered if that huge lump in his faded jeans was for real or if it was just something in his pockets. Finally work was over, and I rushed home to shower and get ready. About 7:30 P.M. Larry knocked on the door. He was wearing a T-shirt, leather jacket, and cutoff jeans. We started with a few beers and some small talk. After about an hour of drinking beer, Larry had to use the john. I watched his tight, round ass in those skintight cutoffs as he walked out of the living room. When he didn't come back, I called out and asked if he was all right. Larry didn't answer at first, then he said, "Come here."

I walked toward the bathroom. Passing by my bedroom door, I saw that Larry was lying on my bed on his back — naked! He had smooth white skin, just a hint of chest hair, and a thick patch of black pubic hair surrounding what seemed to be at least a ten-inch dick. Without missing a beat I walked over to him and bent over to kiss him. He pulled me on top of him, his huge rod pressed between our bodies, rolled me over, and started to undress me. I lifted my hips when he got to my pants, and as he pulled them down, my joystick jumped straight up. A look of surprise crossed Larry's face when he realized that he'd met someone who was *almost* his match.

He sucked my cock for what seemed like thirty minutes, stopping every time I was about to come. He said he wanted to fuck me, with me on top, sitting on his dick, so he could beat my meat while he fucked my ass. It took some doing, but I finally got his ten inches up my ass and started to pivot up and down on his thick pole.

The sound of Larry's huge dick popping in and out of my ass was driving me crazy. He was leaking precome like crazy and using his fist on my dick. I was dripping too, all over his stomach. We fucked like animals until I could tell by Larry's moans that he was about to come. He let go a flood of cream up my ass just as I shot my load all over his chest and face. The force of his spurting tool in my hole made me shoot high enough to hit the wall behind my bed.

Afterward, as we tried to catch our breath, I thought about what a good fuck Larry was; I hated that it was over already. Then I felt him moving around on the bed, and when I turned over to look, I saw that Larry's dick was standing at attention. In no time at all I was just as hard as he was. We kissed and hugged, then Larry asked me to mouth-fuck him.

I got on top of him, my knees straddling his head, and slapped his face a few times with my oversize flesh pole. I got up on my toes and fingertips and started to fuck his face while he beat his donkey dick. I was so hot, it didn't take long before I was ready to shoot again. When I felt myself getting close, I worked my way back down Larry's body, took both our dicks in my hand, and worked them until we shot together. The sight of two huge dicks shooting their loads was too much. Come was absolutely everywhere!

After we came back down to earth, Larry took a shower. I washed up while he got dressed. When I came back out of the bathroom, Larry gave me his phone number and address. I walked him to the door and, kissing him good night, lost control again. I got down on my knees and sucked off that big dick one more time as he leaned against my front door. He shot a small, tasty load in my mouth, then pulled me up and told me to spit his come onto my dick. I let what I had left drip out onto my shaft, and Larry jacked me until I was ready to shoot. When I gasped, "I'm gonna come!" he dropped to the floor, and I let go all over his forehead and the door.

I cleaned off his face with a paper towel from the kitchen. We kissed again (I could still smell my come on him) and made plans for Saturday night. Believe it or not, Saturday night was even hotter!

Pacific Overtures

I have known Paul for three years. He is the product of two distinct races. From his Polynesian forefathers he inherited a tall, solid, muscular build; jet-black hair; gleaming white teeth; and a deep, natural tan. From his European ancestors he inherited a pair of the most extraordinary blue eyes you've ever seen. Being a bisexual in the U.S. Navy, he's always been slow to share the details of his life with others, so it took me quite a while to gain his trust. If his sexual preference were ever revealed, his naval career could be ruined. Over the years, however, we've had some pretty amazing sexual encounters, but nothing equaled last Saturday night.

Lately I've been in the habit of leaving a key out for Paul so he can come by and enjoy the pool while I'm at work. On Saturday I arrived home and found him sitting in a lounge chair, wearing my Japanese bathrobe. I knew he would be wearing one of my G-strings underneath, especially when he asked me to put one on myself as I was changing out my work clothes.

A joint helped me unwind from a busy night in the restaurant. When I looked over at Paul's magnificent body, I could no longer restrain myself. I knelt in front of him as he sat in the chair and slowly untied the sash of the robe, rolling back the folds of fabric to expose a white G-string, which stood out in bold contrast against his beautifully tanned, muscular body.

117

jack hart

I ran my hands up the inside of his legs, over his chest, and down his stomach until they came to rest on his swollen crotch. With feathery strokes I caressed his bulging manhood. A low moan escaped his lips as I eased his legs wider apart and ran my tongue over the well-packed G-string.

"I'd love a massage," Paul murmured. Remembering our last experience with massage oil, I stood up to prepare the room. Paul ran his hands over my body and tongued my cock; it was straining to be released. Upstairs we put towels on the floor, and with lights dimmed and John Klemmer's sax whispering seductively from the stereo, I commenced to oil his back.

I leaned over and rubbed his muscular shoulders, pushing my rock-hard cock against his body — I knew he loved the feel of it. I slowly massaged his back with my whole body, allowing my cock to slide up and down his spine. I pushed my cock between his flexed buns, and another low moan escaped his lips.

I rolled off and turned Paul over to find his rigid member glistening with precome. He slowly rose from the towel, slightly spreading his legs and exposing his glory of glories to me. His body glistened. I rose to meet him, and he guided my cock into him. Slowly I rocked back and forth, each thrust moving deeper and deeper inside him. "Harder, harder," he whispered. But I refused to rush. Gradually I built up the pace until I was greeting his gyrations with long, deep thrusts of my swollen cock. Paul groaned, and I felt his muscles clamp around my cock as he came.

Even though I didn't come myself, this was one of our truly great sexual experiences. It was orgasmic enough for me just to give him pleasure and satisfaction.

The destroyer on which Paul serves left this week for a long cruise. When he's in his bunk at sea and closes his eyes, he can relive this Saturday night, and I know I'll do the same.

118

The Merger

It had been another grueling business meeting. Those eight-hour coffee-drinking, mind-bending marathons really drained me. Or rather, they filled me up. With a distended bladder, I took the motion to adjourn as a signal to head for the head to lighten my load.

Standing in front of the urinal, I waxed poetic in my thoughts, comparing the relief I was experiencing to the relief of tension built up from the day's meeting.

Mike came in and stood at the urinal beside me just as my flow subsided.

"A real pisser," he offered.

"Yeah, in more ways than one," I replied. "Let's unwind with a *cerveza* down at the lobby bar." I looked into the Texan's steel-blue eyes to avoid glancing down to a part of Mike's anatomy that held much more interest for me.

I didn't care much for blonds or married men, but there was something about this one that captivated me. Maybe it was the fact that Mike was the only decent-looking male in an otherwise unremarkable group. Maybe it was that Mike had a strange combination of strength and vulnerability. Or maybe it was just that these out-of-town business trips every other month stirred my desire to get out and romp, and Mike looked like the best available candidate.

119

jack hart

We didn't speak on the way down to the bar, and when the waitress came we ordered chilled mugs of draft beer and then quaffed them over small talk. The second round came and was consumed. At the end of the third beer, I was again in need of relief. "I gotta piss," I said. Mike followed.

In a rest room off the lobby, I stepped up to one in a long row of unoccupied urinals. Mike took the one next to me. We were again side by side even though there were plenty of others available. This fact was not lost on me as my cock began to swell in my hand, slowing my flow. I looked down at Mike's pecker and saw that a similar situation was developing.

Mike grinned. "Looks like we both have a problem. Let's go up to my room and talk." I winked and nodded.

Alone again in Mike's hotel room, we stood facing each other, separated by only a foot or so. I slowly raised the back of my hand to touch Mike's bulging crotch.

Mike stripped and undressed me. I shuddered in anticipation as I lay back on the bed and opened my arms wide. The black hairs on my flat stomach twitched as Mike ran his hands over my pecs and down to my erection. He grasped my nuts with one hand and my solid cock with the other. His grip was firm, stretching my scrotum pleasurably.

Mike rolled his fingers over the head of my cock, spreading the slick precome over its ample surface. He reached for one of the packets of rubbers, tore it open with his teeth, and rolled the satiny prelubricated sheath over my cock.

Next Mike rolled over facedown on the bed, hunched up slightly, and pushed his tight, round buns invitingly upward. I straddled his legs, grasped his ass with both hands, and massaged the firm globes. His flawless ass was covered with an even coat of feathery, slightly curly blond hair. I tongued the inviting crack and nibbled on his tense butt, making Mike moan slightly. Spreading the cheeks before me, I gazed at the tight pucker.

Grabbing a bottle of lotion, I squirted some into Mike's crack and massaged his buns to work the thin water-based lube in.

120

I pushed a finger through the crack into the waiting hole, causing him to arch his back slightly and squeal with surprise. I pushed farther through his pulsing asshole into his rectum and found the round, hard form of Mike's prostate. Gentle massage brought more fluid into Mike's cock. It filled his foreskin and made a wet spot on the sheet as it dripped out. With my free hand I rubbed the precome onto Mike's cock while continuing to milk his insides.

While stroking his cock into taut readiness, I poured more lube over my finger and worked it into his bung hole. Pulling down slightly on the hole and pointing the way with my finger, I slipped my cock into the ready receptacle. We bucked and fucked, bringing each other to the verge of orgasm and then slowing to extend the session as long as possible.

Finally Mike rolled us both over, and without letting me pull out, he sat upright, pivoted on my cock, and lay forward on my soaked hairy chest. Mike's cock had lost some of its rigidity in the heat of the ass fucking, but its substantial length lay heavy on my stomach and pushed into my navel. Before I was aware of what Mike was doing, I felt the rigid head of a dildo pressing against my cock in his ass. Slowly Mike inserted the rubber tube alongside my rock-hard cock. I saw a grimace of pleasure and pain on his face as his asshole contracted and then expanded to receive the additional presence.

Mike sat upright and began to ride the two rods inside him. The sensation of a second brotherly cock fucking alongside mine was something I had never experienced before. It was wonderful! Mike was obviously following along because his bucking movements became more and more enthusiastic.

Come erupted like a bolt of lightening from my cock into the ballooning receptacle of the condom. The intense electricity of my orgasm shot into Mike's prostate, stimulating a hands-free orgasm for him. As he writhed in the convulsion of his own discharge, I saw the thick, creamy load fling from his cock onto his sweat-soaked chest. Both my cock and the dildo popped out of

Mike's ass simultaneously, stretching it in one last, well-timed sensation and stimulating a final explosion of come that hit me under the chin and ran down my neck and onto the sheet.

We lay collapsed, drained of breath, sweat, and other bodily fluids. We lay silently, facing the ceiling with our eyes closed. After a while Mike sighed and said, "Mmm, I think I'm gonna look forward to these business trips in the future."

"Me too, Mikey. Me too."

The Interview

I'm the media director of a large Madison Avenue advertising agency, and recently I was responsible for hiring the new assistant. I'm not much for interviewing people, so I turned the job over to a friend of mine in personnel. She would make the unofficial decision — on the sly, of course — and just run the rest by me for looks.

Late Friday afternoon, about ten minutes till 5, she buzzed me in my office and said that she had a live one. He had tons of experience and was willing to go for the salary I was offering. I asked her to shoot him by right away.

I was preoccupied, riffling through some market surveys, when I heard a rap on the door. I told him to come in and without looking up said, "Take a seat." A few minutes went by, and though I didn't look at him, I could smell his cologne. Paco Rabanne. My favorite. I took a little extra time, enjoying the scent, afraid that I would be sorely disappointed when I saw his face. I wasn't.

He was the kind of guy that not everyone would find attractive, but he was just my type: a Michael J. Fox look-alike. Short, maybe five foot five, with neatly groomed brown hair. Little tufts of it hung down, and he kept sweeping it back with the palm of his hand as he spoke. He was young, maybe twenty-two or so, but he had an air of confidence that belied his age.

123

jack hart

He was dressed in a conservative blue suit with a pale yellow tie. In his lap rested a leather briefcase.

He handed me his résumé, and I silently congratulated Paula in personnel. She sure knew how to pick 'em. He was enrolled in some design classes at night and had about four years in public relations. He was damn near perfect for the job — and a few other things I had in mind.

I could tell he was a little nervous, so I asked him to loosen his tie and relax. He looked grateful. His credentials were in order, so I set about finding out more about him personally.

He told me he lived alone (couldn't stand roommates) and hoped to take over my job one day. I smiled at his honesty, and that opened him up. From then on we talked about lots of things.

It turned out we had a lot in common. We liked the same movies, books, foods, and people, and we both hated bumper stickers of all kinds, polyester polo shirts, and cars with automatic transmission.

To be perfectly honest, I wanted him working under me — literally. Being in a position of management, I had to watch what I did and said carefully. And besides, I'd fallen into that trap before. I get to know a guy as a friend, we have a good time, and then he turns out to be a lousy lay or a total asshole about it, and the friendship is flushed down the john. As much as I liked him and wanted him, I had to watch my step.

Luckily, he made the first move. He probably figured he had nothing to lose and maybe something to gain. It started with some suggestive talk.

"Have you read any good books lately?" he asked me.

"Some. I don't get much time for reading."

"Me neither. I like to read in bed."

"Same here. It's usually the only quiet time I can find."

"Hmm," he said, looking at me with his head cocked and sort of bent forward. "I don't believe that for a minute."

This kind of banter went on for a while. He was definitely talking out of his cock, and I was thinking with mine.

"Well," I said, finally breaking the spell. "It looks like you'd be a real asset to this company."

"You haven't seen all my assets yet," he said seriously.

"Let's have a look then," I challenged.

I wasn't prepared for what happened next. He started talking about skills that definitely had no place on a résumé. And while he talked to me, he started to undress. At first he started slowly with his shirt buttons. Then he really got into it and unbuckled his belt.

"Do you think you can use a man like me?" he asked coyly as he withdrew his throbbing meat from his shorts.

I gasped at the sight of his cock. It was beautiful. The skin was very pale and clear, there were no bumps, and the veins were very faint. It looked almost like a photo that had been air-brushed.

"I certainly think so," I answered.

He got up from his chair and pushed the papers off my desk, taking their place only inches from my drooling tongue. He kicked his shoes off onto the floor and stood on his knees in front of me. His twitching, swollen cock bounced near my lips. With one even, swift movement, he grabbed my head and thrust it onto his waiting pole.

At first I thought I was going to gag. His dick wasn't enormously long, but it was stout, and it came as a total surprise to my throat muscles. He withdrew only slightly to keep me from throwing up. Then it was right back in again.

I deep-throated his raging meat, massaging it and drawing the first drops of come up the shaft from his balls. Like a starving dog, I lapped at his boner, furiously sucking his rod.

Out of the corner of my eye, I could see him as he gyrated his hips back and forth, quickening his pace. He seemed to be oblivious to me; his head was thrown back, and deep, guttural noises emanated from his mouth.

I released my hold on his ass cheeks and began searching out his love hole. It was sweaty and loose already, waiting for my

125

assault. I pried his cheeks apart and pierced his insides with two fingers. I could feel him tighten, and soon he was backing out of my mouth, pushing his hot little butt farther down my fingers.

Determined to bring him off, I fucked him harder from behind while he plowed my face with his meat. I could feel his thighs quivering and shaking: I knew it wouldn't be long.

Then he shot his luscious load down my throat. One huge wad after another lubricated my mouth, and I hungrily swallowed every last drop.

Standing on his knees before me like a god, he looked soulfully into my eyes and then reached down to kiss me, tasting his own juices.

"Not a bad job," he said, winking. "And a hell of a fringe-benefits package. I'll take it."

What a team.

Backseat Driver

About halfway through my last semester at the University of Florida, Gainesville, my grant dried up. It was the coveted Mr. and Mrs. Alexander Jarrell "Get Your Ass Into College, Boy" scholarship, and naturally, I had no other choice but to accept it.

It had always been my parents' dream for me to attend college. Not for family honor, not because they wanted me to be the first Jarrell to get a college education, but because my mom wanted something to talk about with her friends and my dad wanted to be sure that when he grew old he'd be supported in the style to which he'd become accustomed.

As I said, somewhere between my trig class and my Elizabethan poetry lecture, I dug into my pockets and found them empty. I cringed at the thought of facing employment, but the prospect of facing my dad was worse. I hit the want ads.

The first ad that caught my eye read, COLLEGE STUDENTS!! EARN EXTRA $$$ BETWEEN CLASSES. CABBIES WANTED. BE YOUR OWN BOSS, WORK YOUR OWN HOURS, STUDY WHEN YOU WANT TO IN THE PRIVACY OF YOUR OWN LUXURY AUTOMOBILE. CALL MACK AT 555-8395. Naturally, I called.

By the end of the day I was cruising the boulevard in my own "luxury automobile." It was a little dented but not bad, all in all. I headed down to Fourth Street — the known cruising area —

127

but didn't have much luck with the men. The only signal I was sending with a bright yellow taxi was that you needed cash to sit with me. I hit the airport instead.

There was the usual assortment of hot-looking businessmen hanging out by the curb. I love guys in suits, their trim waists and firm little butts well accented by $700 Italian threads. Then there were the vacationers: tanned, healthy, sun-kissed bodies that were mine for the taking. It was a tough choice, but I settled on a hunky-looking young guy with an overstuffed duffel bag. He looked to be about my age, and I knew that if he were a college student, I probably wouldn't get away with a tip — at least, not in cash.

He was about five feet eight inches tall and sported a tousled mop of blond hair. His face and body were deeply tanned, and I guessed he'd been spending time down south. He wore skimpy white jogging shorts that clearly advertised the bulge in his crotch. A black cotton tank top hugged his massive pecs and shoulders, and when he lifted his bag into the backseat, I stared in awe at the rippling muscles in his forearms.

"Barker House," he said when he got into the cab. That was a frat house near the apartment I lived in. I decided against telling him that I was a student too.

"So where are you returning from?" I asked, trying to make small talk. "Miami?"

"Nah, L.A.," he answered.

"Any good?"

"Not really. No action. Might as well have stayed home." As we talked I watched him in the rearview mirror. He was checking me out as much as he could without seeing what I really had to offer. He leaned forward. "Anything going on around here?"

"Could be," I said. "What're you looking for?"

"Ten inches," he blurted out. I could see him smirking in the backseat, waiting for my reaction. I tried to keep a poker face, but I was beginning to shift around in the seat. He had definitely awakened my sleeping cock.

"That so?" I asked and unwittingly glanced down at my own growing basket.

"Yeah," he sighed and leaned back into the seat. He began stroking his crotch through the tiny shorts as he talked. "You know what I usually do with ten inches?" He lifted his strong tanned legs onto the seat.

"What?" I stammered. My cock was growing bigger by the second, due in no small part to the sound of his husky, low voice whispering behind my ear.

"I usually put my hand over the bulge, you know? Right over the shorts without taking them off. It's kinda hard but not quite all the way. The head is poking through the top of the shorts, trying to get out to me, but I make it wait. I stroke the outline of the shaft through the fabric, tracing the length, only it's not so long because it's still doubled up in the shorts."

I straightened up in my seat, trying to keep my eyes on the road. It was like I'd just taken some Sominex: All I wanted to do was sit back, close my eyes, and enjoy it. He was almost fully reclined and still rubbing his cock. I licked my lips and ached to get a better view.

"I pull the shorts down a little so the piece can stretch out some. Now it's almost completely hard." He started breathing heavily. "The nuts are hot and wet and sweaty. I put my face down near the crotch and inhale. Ah, it's sweet! My hot breath makes the balls tingle and jump a little. They want to be sucked, but not yet.

"Instead, I mouth the cock, still in the shorts. It jumps. It's sticking an inch, maybe two, out of the waistband. I blow on it lightly and then lick just the top. I can taste the precome. It's salty, but I love it. I swirl my tongue around the head. Now it's almost blood-red and fully engorged."

It was getting impossible for me to drive. I looked down at my own tool, now rock hard and begging for some action. I hurriedly drove down a side street where there wasn't much traffic. I was going only about twenty miles per hour. I wanted this to last. The guy in the back didn't even seem to notice I was there. It was like I was spying on him.

"Yeah," he moaned. I rose up in my seat a little and looked at him in the mirror. His cock was out, and he was rubbing his balls with one hand and had slipped the other under his shirt to tweak his nipples.

"So I take the shaft in my hand. It's moist from sweat and come. I don't need to spit on it or anything. It's waiting for me. I grab it tight, but not too tight, and run my palm up and down over the shaft. I can feel the veins as they grow. Little cock hairs down near the nuts are tickling me. I take the tangerine-size ball sac in my hand and play with the balls, bouncing them around a little. They try to draw up tight, but I gently pull them back down again, slipping my finger across the skin that leads to his asshole.

"He's shaking now — no, he's trembling. I know I'm driving him crazy, and I don't want to stop. But I gotta taste him. I lower my face toward his oversize basket and take his nuts into my mouth. They're huge, and at first I can take in only one at a time. But I work at it: gargling them in my mouth, licking the sweat and juice off them, flossing my teeth with the little wiry pubes. I open wider and take in both balls. My wet tongue runs over them, covering every inch of their glorious fullness. I know they're packing one helluva load, but I want to coax that cream out of them slowly."

My driving was getting worse by the second. I took the wheel in one hand, but I was afraid to even touch my cock for fear I'd shoot then and there. I started rubbing my pubes in a circular motion, slowly easing down toward my rock-hard tool.

"His cock is jumping," he continued. He was talking so softly, I had to turn off the two-way radio so I could hear. I rolled my window up to block out all other sounds. The whole time, I kept one eye on him in the mirror.

"So I take it. I take it all quickly, sucking and licking, blowing it like a Hoover. I use his balls as a handle and jam his cock farther into my throat. My teeth nick him a few times, but he doesn't care. Hell, he doesn't even notice. I deep-throat him down to his balls, filling my mouth with all ten inches. He starts bucking and moaning, begging me. So I go down on him harder, as hard as I can. He mouth-fucks me and grabs my hair to hold me in place. He doesn't want to let me go. I don't even gag once. His cock is sopping and slick and slides down me with ease. In and out. In and out. In and out. Oh, yeah! I can taste it. He's coming!"

I looked back quickly for fear I was missing something. He was writhing on the seat behind me, completely oblivious to the raging hard-on I was sporting in the front seat. He was lost somewhere, deep in his fantasy. I envied the man with him in his dreams. My own dick was dribbling like crazy, anxiously awaiting his moist, hot mouth.

"I back off quickly. I don't want him to come yet. Instead, I push him back till he's lying flat. I rub the insides of his thighs, massaging him. Then I lift his legs up over my shoulders. His cock is pointing straight at his face, and that's the way I want it. I want him to shoot into his own mouth. I spread his cheeks gently and nuzzle the crack. It's hot and a little damp. I know what treasures await me in that glorious, dark hole.

"I start slowly, just licking his cheeks, fingering his hole. But he wants more and starts begging me. I spear him once with my tongue. Twice. He's screaming now. 'Yes!' he says. 'Give me more!' So I give it to him. I eat his ass out like a starving man. Chewing on the skin, shoving my stiff tongue into his guts. Eating him out. Yes, he loves it."

It was too much for me. I pulled over into an alley and yanked my cock out of my shorts. We jacked off in unison, each thrilling to the scene that was playing itself out in this guy's mind. I tried to imagine him with me. I imagined he was doing it to me, and I could almost feel him rimming me.

I could feel my ball sac crawling its way up toward my hardened cock. The heat in the cab was intense, and our heavy breathing started to fog up the windows. I cranked the window open just a little to let in some air. He continued.

"Still, it's not enough for him. He wants more. Pretty soon he's whimpering and crying, 'Fuck me, please fuck me.' I oblige. Crawling up his hot sweaty back, I can feel my belly sticking to his rippling muscles. He flexes backward and shoves his ass up to my cock.

"It's pointing straight at his slick hole. I don't need to grease my rod because his ass is all wet and slippery from my tongue. I grab hold of my cock, and for a second it feels like its gonna shoot right then.

"I let go and give it a breather. Then I grab it quick and shove it in. I wanna squirt inside him. His gut is warm and liquid. His sphincter closes up immediately around my pud. It grabs it tight as I move in and out. I watch the skin around his asshole grip it tighter with each thrust.

" 'Fuck me!' he screams. Again and again I pound into his tight little butt, ramming my hot meat clear up to his chin. I can't keep it up any longer, I'm there…I'm there. I gotta hold on just one more minute, just another second or two, and he'll be…"

I could feel the man's face getting hot and flushed. I could feel the heat that he was emanating from the backseat. In that one instant I could feel my own cock up his perfect ass, plowing him, pushing him further than he'd ever been pushed before. He continued.

"He's ready. He's about to shoot. I give him a last spearing and then take his aching balls back into my mouth. With my hands I stroke his cock a few quick times. It's too much for him. He screams. And then he shoots. Again. And again."

He shot all over the backseat just as I was unloading on the dash. We were breathing heavily, erratically. I shuddered and tilted the mirror down so I could watch him. He was rubbing his juice all over his stomach, slowly stroking his cock again.

"Four or five big spurts straight up at his face. He licks it off his chin and lips, just like a baby. He's almost crying. I crawl up his body and slurp up the rest. Then I kiss him, and we become one. Oh, yeah!"

After that he didn't speak and almost seemed to be sleeping. I quietly started the car and headed off for Barker House, wondering what he would say to me when he opened his eyes again.

We pulled up in front of his frat house, and I turned around in the seat. His legs were still spread outward, and his hand slowly massaged his stomach.

"Eight-fifty," I said.

"Huh?" He woke, surprised but not embarrassed.

"Eight-fifty," I said again.

He checked his pockets and looked at me with mischievous eyes. "You wouldn't consider taking it out in trade, would you?"

Old Acquaintance

I t isn't easy being in love with your best friend, especially
when he's straight. For as far back as I can remember, I've
yearned to be with P.J. When we were kids nobody knew
anything about my true desires. I had a jack-off buddy who I
fooled around with, but he wasn't P.J. I remember trying to con-
vince my buddy that we should widen our circle of JO friends
by inviting P.J. to join us. Reluctantly he agreed — after all, he
didn't want to be thought of as anything less than the young
straight dude he was supposed to be. Unfortunately, although
P.J. listened to our proposal, he never took us up on it. Still, I
was determined to do whatever it took to bring P.J. and me
together as more than just pals.

On a group trip one year I found myself in an interesting situation. There were four guys but only three beds. We decided to
take turns sleeping in the largest bed with someone else. I
worked it so I'd be paired with P.J. when it came to my turn in
the double. Meanwhile, being under the influence of destabiliz-
ing hormones, I carefully watched where we tossed our clothes
each night before we went to bed. When the lights went out, I'd
get P.J.'s shirt and bury my face in it. My rigid cock was testa-
ment to the intoxicating effect P.J.'s scent had on me. Every
morning the shirt would be back on the floor, just where he'd
thrown it.

The night we were supposed to share the double bed, I must've been blessed because P.J. had had a few more beers than usual. When we called it a night, he stripped down to his briefs, which he probably wouldn't have done had he been sober. His young lean body was so exciting to me.

Capping his firm chest were two pert brown nipples surrounded by a light dusting of hair. Below that was a feast for the eyes: the silky-smooth skin of his washboard stomach. A patch of hair fanned down from his navel to the uncharted territory of his white cotton briefs. In that moment, now locked in my memory many years later, I recall seeing one of P.J.'s nuts resting at the loose leg band of his worn briefs. The sight gave me an erection long before we got into bed.

P.J.'s legs were a vision to behold. Pillars of solid masculine muscle, they were covered from groin to ankle in a thick forest of dark hair, as were his forearms. He was (and still is) truly a man's man — at least, this man's man.

I followed his lead and stripped to my briefs, but I was much quicker to bed in order to hide the swelling in my crotch. I had a restless sleep, to say the least, lying beside the man I'd become so attracted to. Nothing separated our naked flesh but a foot or so of space and some cotton briefs. But I was more than happy to simply bask in the heat from his body.

Hours passed, and I had many thoughts and desires. I finally decided to act on one. P.J. was lying on his side with his back to me, so I reached under the covers and moved my open hand toward his buttocks. I was shaking like a leaf. I felt the expanse of his cotton-covered ass. I envisioned his ass covered in the same thicket of hair that covered his legs, but I couldn't tell for sure. My hand slipped down past his briefs to his leg. Once I felt the soft fur there, my straining cock twitched. I thought I'd cream in my shorts. The contact made P.J. stir, so I feigned sleep. He turned over, and I knew he was probably staring at me, but I didn't flinch. I didn't want to cause a scene. And that's as far as it went — at least that night.

jack hart

P.J. and I are all grown-up now, but we're still the best of friends. And although he's married and has kids, ultimately we did share some pretty exciting moments.

One particularly memorable experience began one night with a few beers (again). It wasn't long before my thoughts returned to my favorite subject: P.J.'s body. He had a few ideas of his own. Once we had a nice buzz, our conversation turned to things sexual. P.J. started talking about fucking women, implying that he wondered what it would be like to fuck a chick up the ass. This was my cue to guide the conversation to my advantage. I didn't have to work very hard; before long P.J. was shyly suggesting that he might like to fuck *my* ass. I was still a virgin, but I was glad to make this sacrifice for him. My only condition was that I wanted to lose my virginity lying on my back.

I began to shake with excitement, and my dick was already hard. We undressed, and P.J. lay on my bed. I knelt between his outstretched legs and lowered my face to his crotch. His cock and balls, snuggled in a dense forest of pubic hair, were still asleep, but I was about to wake them.

I stuck my tongue beneath P.J.'s cock and lifted it from its matted nest, exposing his balls. Then I licked his furry sac until it was drenched with spit. Working my way back to the underside of P.J.'s cock, I massaged it with my lips, careful not to put it in my mouth until it was straining to be engulfed. I slipped my hands under P.J.'s body and cupped his hairy ass cheeks.

With his butt in my hands and his dick three times bigger than when we had begun, I took his cock head between my lips and swallowed him whole. He twitched with excitement. I raised and lowered his hips with my hands, using slow thrusts to build sexual intensity and satisfy my craving. When I felt him swell up even bigger, I let his cock pop out of my mouth. Moving my hands from P.J.'s ass, I slid them over his body, relishing the feel of his smooth flesh. I was overcome with the urge to chew his nipples. Although he gave no immediate response, P.J. seemed to enjoy my touch.

136

When we positioned ourselves to fuck, P.J. surprised me. As soon as we had traded places, with me on my back and P.J. above me between my legs, I felt a warmth around the head of my cock. I looked down to see P.J. sucking me. It lasted no more than a minute, but the gesture made my feelings deepen and my cock throb. We never discussed this, and it never happened again in any of our other too-rare sexual encounters.

P.J. grabbed the lube and slathered some on his rigid cock. I took a handful and greased my virgin hole. When he was slick and ready, he grabbed my ankles and lifted my legs up to expose the bull's-eye into which he was about to thrust his dart. I assumed responsibility for holding this position so he could free his hands to guide his swollen cock into my tight ass. I remember the bulging cock head pushing against my puckered hole. He pressed forward, and I tightened in response. He pulled back and pressed forward again as I relaxed, his cock continuing its slow, smooth entry into my body. I recall the slow stretch of my sphincter and the sudden pop of my asshole around the swollen head. Then P.J. fell forward and filled my hole.

All my apprehension about taking it up the ass had been a waste of time. We fit together like a lock and key. I closed my eyes briefly and concentrated on the thought of us. I pictured him hulking over me, his strong, hairy arms braced on both sides of me. I felt his engorged cock filling me, moving in and out. I heard his shuddered breath. Then I truly understood what it meant for me to consummate my love. I opened my eyes and gazed upon P.J.'s beautiful body. Now I could watch the rhythmic motion he'd established. His tenderness made my first anal experience one I'll always treasure.

After a few more strokes, the rhythm changed. P.J. was thrusting deeper and deeper. His moves became slower but more determined. With my hands on his sturdy lats, P.J. gasped as he unloaded inside me. This continued for about three or four more thrusts. His grip on me weakened, and P.J.'s body relaxed, but he didn't allow himself to collapse on top of me. His head hung near mine, so with a gesture that felt natural to me, I kissed his neck. I was momentarily lost in the experience and blinded by passion. He wasn't taken aback; as a matter of fact, I think he was consumed with thoughts of what had just taken place.

His cock slipped out of me as it softened, and soon he was up and off the bed wiping himself with a towel. We were both quiet, me basking in the afterglow and P.J. probably punishing himself for having indulged. After about ten minutes we said good-bye. When he was gone, I stroked my cock a few times and shot an explosive load.

The next day I made a special point of stopping by P.J.'s house. I didn't want to avoid him or give him time to turn this event into something negative in his mind. When we were together I said, "I had the most wonderful dream last night."

He said, "Oh, yeah?"

"Yeah," I said. "I dreamed that you fucked me. It was so real-istic, I'm sore!"

As I mentioned, we've had several sexual experiences since then, but none involved anal sex or the special passion we shared that unforgettable night.

Close Physical Contact

I reported to my reserve unit's annual training exercises ahead of everyone else. I got a room that, because of my grade as a senior noncommissioned officer, I expected not to have to share. But I returned to my room that first evening to find the other bed covered with clothes and uniforms; I'd been stuck with a second lieutenant.

He was all right, I guess: about twenty-three, wiry but muscular, cute — but married. We'd worked together before, but he'd always been a bit standoffish, and I didn't want to try to force friendship on him. When someone doesn't want to be a friend, it isn't worth the time and effort. Besides, I don't particularly care for married men.

Over the duration of our stay, we discovered that we had very different lifestyles. I usually came in before he did and was in bed by the time he and some of the other enlisted men came back from drinking. One night he was so drunk, I had to give him directions to the bathroom. He was headed first for my closet and then for his before I got him into the head. He pulled the door but didn't close it, so I got all of the sounds. Luckily, he hit the commode instead of the floor. After he straggled back to his bed, he said, "Thanks, Jerry." My name's John.

For nearly two weeks we sort of avoided each other. Whenever we were both in the room and he would have to change, he

139

would go into the bathroom. Only that one time when he had trouble finding the bathroom had I ever seen him in his underwear. But that was soon to change.

He'd had duty this one night and didn't get in until 0130 hours. He was noisy as usual and woke me up. I heard him drop his uniform on the floor and push the rest of his clothes off the bed. He lay down, and I tried to go back to sleep since I had a long drive to make in just a few hours.

I heard him get up, and it sounded like he was crossing the room toward me. I wondered what he was up to. I was starting to roll over when he sat down next me. "John," he said softly, "do you want to make love?"

"What?" I couldn't believe what I thought I'd heard.

"Never mind."

He got up. I turned quickly and grabbed his wrist. He turned back to look at me, his face aflame with embarrassment. It was then that I noticed that he had taken off his T-shirt: He had a beautifully muscled chest, which was covered with a light mat of dark hair. He tried to tug his arm away, though not very convincingly. I sat up and swung myself around so that I was sitting facing him, his boxers looming squarely in my face. "What did you say?" I repeated.

"Nothing."

With my right hand I touched his left nipple through the hair on his chest. He trembled. I touched his right nipple, and he trembled again. I knew then that he wouldn't try to escape. I placed both hands on his hard chest and ran them down to his waist, then tugged on the elastic of his boxers and lowered them to his knees. I gently touched his rapidly inflating cock and rolled his balls between my thumb and forefinger. He moaned softly while I stroked him hard.

I stood up and backed him toward his bunk. He stood there, his boxers around his ankles. I took the blanket from my bed and spread it on the floor, then stripped off my shirt and boxers. Together we lay down.

140

"Just follow my lead," I whispered, and he nodded. Straddling his stomach, I reached up to the nightstand and removed two rubbers from my wallet, then rolled one on myself. I moved down his body, grabbed his cock, and put the other on him. Then I turned him over and grabbed both wrists. He didn't move as I pulled some Vaseline from my gym bag, spread his legs, and applied the jelly to his ass. I lay on his back, my cock in the cleft between his butt cheeks, and humped him without breaching his hole. Within moments I was spent, the head of the rubber full.

I rolled him over onto his back again and slid down his body, ending up astride his legs. I reached for his cock, which remained engorged with passion, and yanked off the rubber with my teeth. He grabbed the legs of the nightstand with both hands as I licked his hairy balls and throbbing cock. Then he shot, his stream arcing up and splattering his chest.

After that we lay together under my blanket for the rest of the night. I left in the morning without waking him, and he transferred out soon afterward.

Military Discharge

I was waiting to board a cross-country military flight when I spotted a Marine Corps gunnery sergeant on the other side of the waiting room. He was about five foot ten, blond, with a stocky build: recruiting-poster handsome — and, at the same time, untouchable. I thought he might have caught me looking his way (we were the last two to cross the tarmac to the plane), but he betrayed no visible interest. How I wanted us to get the last two seats together!

To no avail. I got the last seat in the rear section, and he got the last seat in the center section. I spent the whole trip making up an imaginary conversation with him — and a bit more.

When we landed in Cherry Point, North Carolina, it was late, and I didn't know how to get to Camp Lejeune. I was talking to a lieutenant I knew from night school about my predicament when the sergeant approached and said that he had missed his flight. Fortunately, there was a housing office nearby that offered the possibility of rooms. "There," said the lieutenant, "your problem is solved." The sergeant had a car pick us up and take us to the housing office, where we were offered separate rooms. He suggested that we share quarters to save on expenses. I just about died. Could this really be happening?

Once settled in our room, we changed, and then he suggested we go into town for dinner and a couple of beers. We found a bar within walking distance that served hot sandwiches, and we wolfed down dinner and a couple of brews there. Around an hour or so later, back to the room we went.

We undressed pretty much in the dark, both choosing to keep on our underwear. I turned away from the sarge, nursing a persistent ache in my gut that wasn't from the spicy meatball sub I had just consumed.

"Would you like to fool around?"

"What?" I asked, certain I had heard him wrong.

"I haven't been with anyone for a while, and I thought that fooling around was on your mind when you agreed to share a room with me," he said, looking at me levelly.

I turned to face him. "It would be my pleasure."

We stepped toward each other. Although the room was dark, a dim light was shining through the closed blinds. He took off his T-shirt as I removed mine, but before he could remove his briefs I stopped him.

"Let me," I whispered, leading him over to the bathroom door and turning on the light. "I want to see what I'm getting." He smiled a smile that would have melted the hardest heart. I knelt in front of him and pulled his underwear down. His uncut cock flopped out as I freed it from his white cotton briefs. He stepped out of his shorts, and I gently eased him back into the light. He was beautiful! His torso was muscular, and a light brown fuzz sprinkled his barrel chest. Foreskin covered the tip of his ample cock, and I ran my tongue around it, teasing the slit. His hands were on my shoulders, rubbing and kneading.

The sarge cupped his hands around my chin and pulled me to my feet. Wordlessly he slipped one arm around my waist and guided me to the space between the beds, where we lay on the floor. I stroked his cock to renewed hardness; the salty taste was inviting as I tongued the precome from his slit. He reached under my briefs and ran his hand over my ass. Then he rolled me from my side to my back, pulled down my briefs, and knelt astride my legs. He leaned over me to reach his wallet, withdrew a condom, tore the packet open with his teeth, and handed the condom to me. I covered his hard, throbbing cock with it.

He raised me up and put a pillow under my back. With my legs over his shoulders but still shackled by the briefs, he entered me slowly. I ran my hands over his hairy chest as he began to sweat from the exertion. He grabbed my cock and jerked it in time with his own plunges. Suddenly he pulled out and ripped the condom off. I grabbed his cock and stroked rapidly, his foreskin sliding up over his cock, then retreating like an ocean wave. I had stroked him only a few times when his body began to tremble. His come exploded like water from a breached dam, laying down a line of white from my chin to my cock. I gulped for air, and he covered my mouth with his. The smells of sweat, beer, and spicy meatballs were heady and overpowering. I gasped and came, and we lay side by side, feeling the warmth of each other's bodies. That night I slept deeply and contentedly.

The next morning we returned to the air terminal, where the sarge caught his flight and I found a ride to Camp Lejeune. We parted with a handshake and a smile.

After the Flood

This was not like any other day I'd ever experienced — at least, outside my fantasies — although it started out the same. My roommate, J.P., and I had gone to the local gym for our daily workout. As usual, I checked out the guys, and J.P. checked out the girls. Today, however, he didn't seem as interested in the girls as he usually was. He seemed strangely preoccupied. I also noticed that he was watching my workout a little more closely than normal, but I didn't think much of it because, after all, he was straight.

After our workout J.P. and I returned home to our quiet two-bedroom apartment. It was my turn to make supper, so I went into the kitchen to get started. J.P. decided his muscles needed a soak in the tub before we ate, so he went off to relax in the bath.

I thought a nice salad and fruit would be filling enough, so I went to work. I was halfway through chopping the lettuce when I heard J.P. yell out, "Paul, help!" I put down my knife and went to the bathroom to see what kind of mischief J.P. was into, and when I got there he was laughing so hard, he could barely speak. Somehow he had managed to get his big toe stuck in the faucet with the water still running. The water was spraying every-where, and because he was laughing so hard, J.P. couldn't sit up enough to get his foot free. After a few minutes I managed to get his toe unstuck and the water turned off, but by then I was as wet

jack hart

as J.P. (not to mention a little excited by seeing his beautiful body totally revealed). Rather than letting him see how aroused I was, I made the excuse that I needed to get out of my soaked clothes, and I headed for the door.

By the time I got back to my room, my dick was rock hard. I sifted through a pile of clothes and decided on a pair of loose-fitting jeans that wouldn't reveal my manhood too much, and I started to peel off my wet clothes. I had gotten only my shirt off when I felt a hand on my shoulder and heard a soft whisper, "Here, Paul, let me help you with those. After all, I need to show my appreciation for your saving me back there." Trembling and thinking I must be dreaming, I turned and faced my roommate.

J.P. calmly put his hands on my waist and responded to my obvious surprise with, "It's okay, I won't bite. I've wanted you for a long time but never had the balls to do anything about it — until now." By the time my head stopped spinning, we were on the bed, covering each other with tender kisses. I didn't realize how real it all was until I got him on his back and removed the towel he'd been wearing. The proof came when I saw his nine-inch cock standing erect, a little soldier waiting for a command. I took his massive meat in my mouth and worked it like no woman ever could. J.P. lay there moaning and arching his back with every stroke of my tongue. I could tell he was getting close to blowing his wad, so I eased off a little, not wanting this to end. After all, it might be the only chance I'd ever get with J.P.

Just when I thought it was over, J.P. reached down and pulled me up. He looked me in the eyes, smiled, and said, "It's my turn." I rolled over as he worked his way down my torso, nibbling and kissing all the way. When he got to my pubic hair, he buried his face, took a deep breath, looked up, and grinned. "You've outdone yourself, Paul," he said. "This is the best meal you've fixed for me yet." With that, he went to work on the hearty piece of meat before him. He sucked and licked like no man I'd ever known, topping off my arousal with a plea for me to fuck his ass.

146

At first I wasn't sure about fucking him since this was his first time with a man, but he insisted that he wanted it, and I've never been able to say no to him. I reached for the K-Y in my nightstand and proceeded to loosen him up as he sucked me off. I signaled that I was ready, and he rolled over to bare his hungry ass to me. As I eased my way in, he looked up and smiled, then reached back and pulled me into him.

It was so nice and warm inside J.P. that I almost lost my load right then. He bucked himself all the way down my shaft, and I began a slow, deep pistoning action. Before I knew it, I was pounding him like a rabbit in heat. To J.P.'s surprise, his dick was throbbing and ready to come without either of us touching it. We both shot our loads at the same time, then sprawled in a heap of flesh and sweat on the bed.

We must have lay there cuddling for an hour or more when J.P. cleared his throat to say something. I braced myself, ready to hear him tell me he'd be looking for a new place to live in the morning, but he didn't. All he said was, "I love you, Paul. Sweet dreams." Then he drifted off to sleep, holding me in his arms. From that moment on, I knew we'd never have separate bedrooms again.

Naked Lunch

Amazing things can happen to you in the most ordinary situations. All you need is a little imagination and a lot of patience.

I've worked at the downtown headquarters of a large insurance company for several years. Most of the staff is your usual assortment of overeducated, overdressed, overfed yuppies. And outwardly I probably resemble them. However, after eight years of working out in a gym four times a week, I can still bench-press 300 pounds — not bad for a thirty-year-old executive.

About two months ago something happened that really changed my attitude toward my work — or at least my lunch hour. One day around noon our receptionist announced that a delivery person had shown up with an ice chest filled with sandwiches, salads, and sodas. I went to the lobby to see what he had to offer. Sitting on top of the cooler was the sexiest man I'd ever seen. He looked to be about twenty-eight years old, with brown hair, gray eyes, and a handlebar mustache. When he stood up to greet me, I could tell from his impressive physique that he must have played football at one time. He had massive shoulders, a broad chest, and thick forearms. A lightweight shirt and short pants highlighted his hairy chest, legs, and arms. He carried his change in a small apronlike pouch that covered his crotch (the importance of this I'll explain later).

When I asked him for a roast-beef sandwich, he seemed eager to find me a fresh one and insisted on digging to the bottom of his ice chest to find the perfect sandwich. I purposely stood back so I could get a good look at his behind. His shirt had come untucked, revealing a trail of curly brown hair that surely extended downward to cover his beautiful buns. When asked for some mustard, he reached into the apron covering his crotch and pulled out a packet. He then asked if I would like any more mustard. I said yes, and this time he fumbled around a little longer in his pouch, finally retrieving three more packets.

Back in my office I forced down the worst roast-beef sandwich I'd ever tasted, but the knowledge that the packets of mustard had been snuggling against his crotch all morning made the sandwich a bit more palatable.

The next day I postponed a meeting just so I could catch the deli man at noon. This time two attractive women from accounting were also checking out his wares. My man was trying to flirt with them, but they ignored him. After they left, he asked about the other women in the office, explaining how "fuckin' horny" he'd been since arriving in Los Angeles two months earlier. He said his wife had left him after he lost his job at a steel mill back in Ohio, so he moved to L.A. for the work. He said he hadn't "plugged anything for three months"; he hadn't even known anyone he could talk to about it, until now.

Then he told me his name was Arnold but that his friends called him Bear. I asked him why. And right there, in the middle of the lobby, he pulled up his shirt. A thick mat of hair covered his stomach. "This is why they call me that," he admitted. "I have this damn pubic hair all over my body. It used to drive my old lady nuts. She hated it."

The next day the same two women were buying sandwiches. Bear was fumbling with his change pouch more than ever. As they walked away, he looked forlorn but continued to fiddle with his apron. When he bent down to get my sandwich from the ice chest, I looked in the pouch and couldn't believe what I saw.

jack hart

Under the packets of mustard was a beautiful uncut cock. It was about half hard. That horny son of a bitch had cut a hole in his pouch and pulled his cock through!

I was determined to have him. The next week our company was sponsoring an all-day picnic off-site. Bear had no reason to know this and would be coming to the office as usual. I scheduled a fake appointment so I could get out of the picnic.

That day I was the only one in the office. I showed up wearing my old gray sweatpants and no underwear so that my cock would be easy to get to. Plus, I was wearing a loose-fitting tank top — in case Bear wanted to get at my pecs.

At 12 noon on the dot, Bear arrived. A puzzled look washed over his face when he saw there was no receptionist. I just happened to be lurking about (ha!) and explained that the office was closed but that I was glad he'd showed up because I needed some help moving furniture. I'd be glad to pay, I added.

As I talked, Bear was fingering his cock through his pouch. Absentmindedly (yeah, right!) I started pulling on my erection through my sweatpants. The conversation stopped for several seconds as we looked into each other's eyes, then down at each other's growing bulges. I led Bear down the hall to my office. I told him I needed some information from the other side of the building and that he should wait and make himself comfortable. He sat on the couch in my office and picked up my new copy of a popular girlie magazine. I closed the door and walked down the hall. After about five minutes I went back to my office. Bear had his back to me, gazing down at the centerfold spread open on the table. He didn't bother to turn around, but he dropped his hands to his side. As I walked around to face him, I realized how physically imposing he was; the sexual tension had my heart beating so fast, I felt light-headed.

This is how I finally got to see the cock I'd been fantasizing about for so long. Bear's cock was the fattest I've ever seen, as fat as a beer can and perfectly straight. I'd guess it to be about eight inches long — the perfect tool for this hairy stud.

150

Bear didn't grab his cock. He knew what he wanted. He looked at me sadistically and growled, "Lick it." The next thing I knew, I felt his bear paws on my shoulders as he pushed my head down to meet his cock. When I got down on my knees, I reached out with my hand for his tool. He slapped it away. "I said *lick it*," he said. I was taken by surprise but understood that Bear was now in control. As I sucked his fat dick, I tried to get it all in my mouth but couldn't because of its immense girth.

Bear then ordered me over to the couch, where he placed my head at the edge of the seat cushion. He pulled off his shirt and pants and again aimed that mighty tool at my face. I was completely at his mercy. He wanted his whole cock in my mouth. He began fucking my face. He must have felt the resistance at the back of my throat, but he kept pounding and pounding, the tempo increasing, and finally I got the entire cock in! Bear pulled it all the way out, then plunged it all the way in again. He growled, "I bet you want some honey from the bear." He forced his cock all the way in and left it there for what seemed like an eternity, then let out a low-pitched moan, and I felt hot jets of come pouring down the back of my throat. The fact that I started shooting without even touching myself helped me overcome my fear of suffocating on his bear cock.

The Test-drive

L ast summer my trusty VW Bug finally blew up on me. I was in Marin County, traveling the windy road from the beach back to my apartment in San Francisco. Suddenly I heard a coughing and a sputtering.

The whole car shook, and as I inched my way up the steep hill, I tried to remember every prayer I'd been taught when I was a boy. But it was no use. After another hundred or so excruciating feet, my long-suffering companion crawled to the side of the road and died.

This, I knew, was the end. I was going to have to buy myself another car.

The mere thought of car shopping sent a chill up my spine. My brother in-law — the one I loathed — was a car salesman, so I knew firsthand what a slimy lot car salespeople are.

I'd been saving in anticipation of this occasion, and I didn't want some sneaky bastard in a mismatched outfit to make off with my $6,000 just like that.

I called my next-door neighbor and had him come pick me up. I could tell he wasn't thrilled with me because he dropped me off right at the car dealership at Alameda and Magnolia.

Sure enough, as soon as I got out of the car, they came at me like a bunch of vultures. Four or five of 'em seemed to crawl up out of the floor and head straight for me.

A little overwhelmed and rather anxious, I ducked into the john to collect my thoughts and adjust my attitude before I faced the pack of bloodsuckers.

As I stood in front of the mirror, taking a piss, a really handsome stranger came out of one of the stalls. He smiled warmly at me and crossed over to wash his hands.

I checked him out in the mirror as I peed. He was a real looker: dark straight hair, a little on the longish side; piercing blue eyes; and the squarest jaw I'd ever seen. His tight little butt flexed as he reached over to get the soap, and I thought I'd cream in my pants right then and there.

I decided he might be an ally and tried to strike up a casual conversation.

"Here to buy a car, eh?" I said nonchalantly.

"Pardon?" He swung around as he wiped his hands dry. His skin was beautiful, and I imagined his masculine hands caressing my aching body.

"Me too," I said. "I'm here to buy a car too. But don't tell those bastards that." I motioned toward the lobby with my hands. "No, if they knew that I'd walked through that door with $6,000 in my pocket, ready to buy a car, they'd rape me — metaphorically speaking, of course."

He grinned. "Of course."

"My old car just crapped out on me. I wish I knew someone else around here so I wouldn't feel at such a disadvantage. Don't know shit about cars."

"Maybe I can help," he said.

"How's that? You a mechanic?"

"No," he replied. "I'm one of those bastards."

I felt my face flushing with embarrassment and would have run out of there as fast as my legs would take me; the only problem was that my dick was still hanging out of my shorts.

"Oh, God. I'm sorry." I went to shake his hand and then realized I'd just been taking a piss. I withdrew my hand, but he looked directly at it and then grasped it tightly.

jack hart

"That's okay," he said. "Let's see if we can get you into an automobile."

We found a model I really liked, and Sam (my dream dealer) told me, with a wink of the eye, that it was $5,999, stripped. That sounded like it had possibilities, and I knew that I was in the right car as we drove away to take a test-drive. Sam squeezed my thigh gently, and I made a beeline for the hills.

It's hard to find a deserted spot in San Francisco, especially in the summer, but I found a place out near the beach. There was some construction going on, so I pulled behind some heavy machinery.

"How's it handle?" Sam asked slyly as I shut off the ignition.

"I'll let you know in a minute," I whispered. Reaching over, I put my hand over the huge mound of his crotch.

"Take it out," he said. "Take it out and suck it."

I obliged. With my teeth I tore open a rubber packet and slid the glove on over his dick without even using my hands (a trick I learned from my next-door neighbor). Once I had his dick completely covered, I took his rod in my hand and squeezed gently, easing the fat pink head into my mouth a little at a time.

Soon the entire length of his shaft was down my throat, pulsing and throbbing against the roof of my mouth and sliding against my teeth.

He moaned softly and took hold of my ears with his slender fingers. Playing with the hair at the nape of my neck, he urged me down even farther until my nose was buried in his pubes.

"I thought you said it was stripped," I murmured between mouthfuls.

"So it is," he replied. Sam unbuttoned his shirt and exposed his furry chest. The thick, curly black hair covered almost every inch of his massive pecs, and I knew I'd have to go hunting for his nipples.

While I sucked him off, he pinched his tits. Through the corners of my eyes I watched as he let his head drop back, losing himself in the ecstasy. He massaged his chest, running his fin-

154

gers lightly down the cleft between his armor-plated tits and then continuing on down to brush against his rippled abs. He was getting me hotter and hotter.

My own throbbing meat was pushed up against the steering wheel. I furiously fought the zipper that confined it in my jeans, and once freed, it sprang upward, its precome juices glistening in the late-afternoon sun. Sam reached over and held it tightly. With tiny, almost imperceptible jerks, he began jacking me off. Soon his motions became long and exaggerated, traveling the length of my veiny shaft from my balls to my cock head.

My nuts drew up tight and prepared for the explosion about to come. Not wanting to shoot before Sam did, I stepped up my pace on his dick. Sucking all the air out, I created a vacuum in my mouth and brought him off to a shuddering climax. He howled and held my cock even tighter as I shot my wad all over the brand-new plastic dashboard.

Spent, we lay sprawled in the front seat, our bodies twisted. Sam pulled me to him and kissed me lightly on the nose. "It's a steal," he whispered.

"I'll take four," I answered breathlessly.

Of course, one was my limit, and as I drove away in my brand-new auto reeking of the unmistakable smell of sex, I looked at the odometer and wondered just how many miles this one would last.

Ménage à Garage

There was a paved alley behind the houses on the street where I used to live. On one side of the alley was a solid row of garages, and on the other side there were a couple of office buildings. One of the buildings was directly opposite the garage behind my house, and next to it was a parking lot illuminated at night by a big floodlight. There were four stalls in the garage. We kept our car in the end stall, and the other three stalls were empty at night. One of the doors always stood open, and the floodlight from the parking lot would shoot a shaft of light into the garage, making a lighted path. The rest of the garage would be absolutely black.

During the summer I'd walk home from work — I was a salesman at a discount hardware store — and I'd go through the garage. Having watched my share of bulging crotches at work, I'd be in desperate need of release, and I'd often step into the dark shadows and have a wild jerk-off session.

I had a regular ritual: I'd unzip my fly, unfasten the button, and open my pants as far as I could — keeping the belt buckled so my pants wouldn't fall. I'd slip my briefs just below my ass and balls so I could get everything out. I'd milk my cock and caress my balls. Then I'd swing my half-hard cock around and stroke it a few times until it was ready to go. If I had enough pre-come, I'd rub it over the head and give it a good massage.

By that time my cock would be hard enough to drive through a metal door. I'd begin with a slow pump, and then I'd push my hips out as far as I could and work my hard piece of meat. I'd barely be able to see it in the dim light. I'd continue for about four or five minutes, and then I'd increase the speed. I'd begin to feel it. I'd gyrate my hips, thrust them out, and moan some more, and finally my dick would explode. I always tried to shoot my load into the light so I could watch it. I usually shot seven or eight feet.

One particular day I was feeling super horny. I should have beaten off before I went to work, but I didn't have the chance. As I worked around the store, staring at guys' crotches, I could feel my dick getting harder in my briefs.

After work I couldn't wait to get into the garage to begin my jerk-off session. I went into the garage shadows, opened my pants, and slid my briefs down. I took my hard pecker in hand. I tried to bend it parallel with the floor, but it hurt. I pumped and moaned a few times.

Then I heard the sound of someone's shoes crunching dirt against the concrete floor. Someone was in there, watching me. It really jolted me. With hard dick in hand, I spit out in a loud stage whisper, "Who's there?"

He answered, "It's okay. I'm friendly."

I could hear him coming toward me, and my dick began to soften. "You got a nice piece of meat there, fella," he said. "Lemme feel it." I dropped my hand, and he took hold of me. "Wow," he said. "You've got a nice big cock. It's huge!"

We were now facing each other, and I put my hand on his dick. I love the feeling of a good stiff pecker in my hand. He had a big one too, with a nice backward curve, and it was plenty hard. We stroked one another's dick for three or four minutes without saying a word.

He took my balls in his other hand and gently squeezed. I could feel my legs beginning to shake and tremble, and I thought I might fall over. Then he stepped back and got down on his knees. He was still stroking my cock, and now it was harder than ever. I could tell he was trying to see it in the dark light. He kissed the head and began licking the base, slowly working his way up to my cock head.

Then I felt his hot, wet mouth engulfing my cock. My whole body went rigid. He took as much in his mouth as he could, and then he began thrusting with his head — up and down, up and down. He tried to deep-throat it, but it wouldn't bend enough, so he got up off his knees and bent his head so he could take the whole thing down his throat.

I lost track of where I was: All that existed was my big stiff cock in his working, sucking, raging mouth. "Oh, yeah. Suck my dick, you cocksucker, eat me!" He was sucking like a mad-man. I could feel my load beginning to boil. "More!" I yelled. "Harder! Faster!"

He obliged. I began thrusting my hips to fuck his face. Then I exploded in that poor fucker's mouth, and I felt like I was going to drive my cock right through the back of his head. I could hardly keep my balance. I could hear him struggling to take my come. He didn't know whether to suck or swallow.

It took me a minute to recover because he kept nibbling on my dick. "Oh, man! That was good," I cooed. "You really love cock, don't you?" But all I could hear was his moaning: My cock was still in his mouth. My dick had begun to soften, and his sucking on it was becoming uncomfortable. So I pulled my cock out of his mouth. I then pulled my handkerchief out of my pocket and began to wipe my dick off.

He stood up, straightened his clothes, and walked out the door — but not before letting out a long, soft wolf whistle.

Joe's Feet

I don't remember exactly when it began, but I've always been attracted to feet. When I was a teenager I'd go to the New Jersey shore and watch the surfers as they came out of the water just to catch a glimpse of their perfectly tanned feet.

The foot is a curious part of the anatomy. It withstands all the daily pressures the male animal imposes on it, and to me, it's a sign of strength. Size doesn't necessarily matter — but shape is important. A man who keeps his feet in good condition attends equally well, or better, to the rest of his body.

Well, a few weeks ago I moved into the second floor of one of Boston's famous triple-decker buildings. I had noticed the hunk upstairs on several occasions as I was moving stuff in. We chatted one day in a casual way, and I found out his name is Joe.

It was summer, so one day I got to see him outside without a shirt. He's blond and obviously spends a good deal of time pumping iron — his pecs and arms are thickly muscled. Still, he was always wearing running sneakers with white socks, which in a way is sexy — but I'd rather have the bare facts.

Last week an envelope addressed to Joe was placed in my mailbox by mistake. So, being the charitable guy that I am, I went upstairs to return it to its rightful owner.

I had fantasized about Joe whenever I heard him walking around upstairs, apparently without shoes from the sound of the footsteps (and maybe even without socks). Well, to my surprise Joe arrived at the door clad in only bikini briefs. His were the best-looking — and among the biggest — feet I'd ever seen!

He'd obviously just had a pedicure because his nails were well-trimmed. His toes were straight but not "bony," and his arches were defined. Joe must have caught me staring because he said, "Wanna come in?" Naturally, I did.

We sat and talked for a while about how I liked living in the area and about other incidental facts. Suddenly he placed his left foot directly on my lap! I sat shocked for a minute. He realized I'd been caught off-guard and said, "I think I need a massage. I was at the gym today and worked out hard."

I began by massaging his soles, then ran my hand up to the toes and worked little circles around each one as I dug my hands deeper into the skin of this erotic body part. He began moaning.

I lifted his left foot to my mouth and began sucking on his toes. I licked the arch while I massaged his right foot with my other hand.

Soon he was opening his fly. He took out one of the largest cocks I'd seen in a long time. He gently jerked it as he commanded me, "Suck my feet, fucker, eat the lowest part of me." His demanding voice made me hard, and for an instant I released my hand from his foot to take my cock out.

He told me to get up and retrieve the bottle of baby oil from the kitchen counter. Then he said, "Stand there with your dick out," and I did. He told me to rub baby oil over the soles of his feet. After I did that, he pressed them against my crotch, cradling my cock and balls between his glistening arches. "You've probably had good hand jobs and great blow jobs," he said, "but this is going to be a super foot job." He wrapped those dogs around my cock so forcefully — using his powerful toes to give me the most incredible massage I've ever experienced — that in eight or nine strokes I was shooting come all over his feet. He commanded me to "lick it all up," and I did. I left those feet cleaner than if he had just taken a shower. I licked up and down his soles, taking each toe into my mouth and eating all the come I had deposited on him.

He'd begun to remove his briefs while I was servicing his feet, and now he jumped up and stripped completely. He led me to a queen-size mattress in his bedroom. I stripped too. He grabbed a tube of Vaseline from the night table and spread a small amount on his hand, then on his cock. He lay on the bed faceup and told me to "face those fuckers," meaning his feet, and to lower my butt onto his hard cock.

I slowly took all nine inches up my ass. Just as I felt the tickly of his bush against my cheeks, I could see him wiggling his beautiful toes. Then he demanded, "Service my feet again," and I happily bent over and began sucking his size elevens as he started fucking my tight ass.

After a while he started clenching his toes, and I knew what was coming — he was! I started tonguing his toes furiously, and he gripped my buns, yelling, "Suck my feet, motherfucker, make me shoot!" just before shooting a huge load of come deep inside me.

At least twice a week now I go upstairs just after Joe has returned from the gym, his feet all sweaty of course. Our ritual begins with my washing his feet and has now advanced to foot fucking. It's quite an improvement over finger fucking!

Ninth-Inning Stretch

It was the top of the ninth, and my bladder was full from eight innings of beer. I left my girlfriend in her seat and went to relieve myself.

In the stadium men's room the urinals are one long trough, which stretches from one wall to the other. Three guys were already standing there when I walked in.

For some odd reason, whenever I drink too much beer and have to piss, I get a hard-on. (I lose my balance too.) I asked myself, *How am I going to piss with a hard-on, and what will these other guys think if they see my hard cock?* But I had to piss before I busted a gut — and besides, I'm always curious to compare endowments.

I unbuttoned my fly and tried to pull my cock out, but it was too hard. So I undid the waist and let my jeans down far enough to stick my cock out over the edge of the trough.

I thought I was being watched because I wasn't pissing — I was just standing there with a semierection. A minute or two passed, and I noticed that the other guys weren't pissing either. The two on my left had hard-ons hanging out of their flies, and the guy to my right was stroking his fat uncut cock. The head was glossy and wet-looking. He pulled his foreskin over the head, concealing it in his paw, then pushed his pelvis forward, exposing the big shining head.

I thought to myself, *What a bunch of show-offs. If these guys think they're big, just wait till they see my cock when it gets throbbing hard!*

So I began to stroke my dick. The veins looked like a road map. My cock stood straight up, parallel to my chest. My pride stretched out ten inches, almost to the top of my stomach.

The other guys gasped. It was such a thrill that I forgot I had a girlfriend waiting for me back in the stands.

I squeezed the tip of my dick, and a clear drop of precome oozed out. I rubbed it around my cock head and polished my stiff tool with it. I felt an ejaculation contraction, but it was just a tremor warning of the real thing.

The guy on my right started breathing heavily as he plunged his cock through his fist. He squeezed his meaty hand around the neck of his cock, and his pet started spitting into the trough. I watched the white stream float down past me — and past the two guys on my left.

I squeezed another big drop of precome from the tight hole of my red, swollen cock. I shined and polished it all over my stiff meat. The guys on my left shot their loads at the same time. They must have been holding their jizz for several weeks at least because they shot load after load after load.

My temples started pounding, my breath got heavier, my heart raced, and I felt those tremors again. By standing on my toes, I was able to hold back as long as I could. But my legs started shaking, and I gave in. My cock sprayed jism all over the wall in front of us. I milked my cock of one thick, creamy wad after another. It was good to the last drop!

I shook the last few drops from the tip of my cock and stuffed it down the leg of my jeans. The announcer called the winning score over the P.A. system. The mob could be heard coming toward the men's room. The other guys zipped up. I went out to find my girlfriend. I wonder if she ever noticed the wet spot on my jeans.

Straight Shot

Well, I decided to make a fantasy come true. I called up this "We Make Videos of Anything You Want" place and asked them to come over.

When they arrived, it was just as I had hoped — two very straight guys thinking I wanted to be taped fucking some chick. I explained, with some embarrassment, that I wanted them to tape me jerking off. They were a little shaken, but when I offered to pay them double, they got over it.

I told them I wanted a video of me wearing only my boxer shorts, doing a long jerk-off session. I stripped down to my shorts and lay on the bed. They started the cameras.

Slowly I caressed my thighs, and though I was on my back, I caressed my buns too. I worked my hand around and stuck it up the right leg of my shorts. I played with my balls, and with my right I pulled on the head of my rapidly growing cock. I was no longer "acting" as I moaned, for the moment had arrived when I could no longer hold back, and I shot a thick load all over my stomach. By now one guy had his prick out and was jerking it while the other watched him and then looked at all that goo on my stomach. I lay completely still.

Well, before I knew what was happening, the second guy straddled my chest, pinning my arms with his legs, and stuck his prick in my mouth while jerking it as fast as possible. The first

164

guy spat on his prick and, pushing my legs up in the air, put it all the way in my ass without a pause. It hurt like hell, but it was worth it.

First the guy in my ass shot — I could feel the hot stuff — and then he went limp and pulled out. The other guy was still jerking into my mouth. Suddenly the one who'd already come took the other guy's hand off his own prick and pushed the thing all the way into my mouth. Then he cupped the guy's balls and squeezed them gently.

The guy in my mouth was in ecstasy. "Oh, God!" he shouted, shooting the biggest wad I'd ever taken down my throat.

Then they both backed off as if they suddenly felt ashamed of themselves. I asked them if they wanted a copy of the tape for themselves. The one who'd been in my mouth said no, adding that he thought they should shoot another tape.

By now they've been back here so often, I'm getting bored. I do the same thing, they do the same thing, and then they leave. Each time I think, *Next time I just won't answer the door.*

But the last time, the guy who fucks me in the ass grabbed my prick and put the tip in his mouth for a few seconds. It felt good to have a "virgin" do that. I figure, *What the hell — they're learning.* So I open the door.

The Buddy System

About ten years ago I got torn up really badly in an automobile accident. I was heading home around 2 a.m. on New Year's Day when my car was hit broadside at the intersection around the corner from my house.

It was just my luck that that was the only New Year's Eve I've ever gone out to party — for exactly that reason. The last way I want to ring in my New Year is by trying to dodge the drunken assholes on the thoroughfare.

Anyway, it landed me in the hospital for about twelve weeks. And let me tell you, that's plenty of time to do nothing but sit around and think. I knew I was lucky to have survived, and while I was laid up, I had an inspiration: To do my part to make sure at least one drunken sod didn't hurt anyone, I decided to volunteer for the emergency-ride program in my city.

As part of the program, a bunch of us guys sit around in the lobby at the Y every New Year's Eve, drinking black coffee and watching David Letterman tapes, waiting to hear from some jerk who's tossed a few too many back to safely navigate an automobile. Actually, that's wrong; they're not the jerks. The ones who *don't* call — they're the assholes.

Anyway, this is where my story really begins. Last New Year's Eve I was sitting around the lobby, waiting for a call. I was the last guy left when the phone finally rang.

166

It was some chick calling from a house on Long Island. She was having a bash, and she thought one of her houseguests had had too much. Everyone else had gone home already, and she couldn't drive him because she had two sleeping kids at home.

When I got there, the guy was still insisting he wasn't drunk, but he respected what we were trying to do for him, so he went along pretty much without a fight.

One look at this guy, and I could see why this woman was so uptight about keeping him alive.

He looked like the studious type; maybe he was an attorney. The fabric covering his fine build must have run at least five bills, and he smelled of the most expensive cologne. I really bagged a hot one that night.

As we drove back toward the city, he rolled down all the car windows and hung his head out. I thought he was going to be sick, but he said he just liked the feeling of the breeze.

Anyway, it gave me a perfect chance to check him out. He stood about five foot eight — not a tall one, but he seemed to be packing that frame with a lot of beef.

His thighs were so thick with cords of muscle that the pants of his suit strained when he squirmed about on the seat. And that flimsy silk was doing very little to hide his delicious basket. It wasn't humongous, mind you, but it looked like the perfect gourmet snack for a cold winter's night.

I tried making conversation with him; I asked him about that dish we'd left back at the house.

I thanked my lucky stars when he told me she was his sister. Then suddenly he blurted out, "I'm gay, you know."

I told him that I hadn't known. But since he was being so truthful, I told him I was too. He just nodded at me kind of sideways and said, "Yeah, I could tell."

Now, that pissed me off a little — his being so cocky and all. When I asked him how he could tell, he pointed right at my crotch and said, "There's no way that could get stiff just by looking at me if you were a straight guy."

167

jack hart

I couldn't believe my luck.

Needless to say, I found us an all-night coffee shop right away. I wanted to get as much of that liquor as I could out of his system. I didn't want a fucking bottle of Chivas to interfere with my New Year's party.

He downed a couple of large ones, and no sooner had we gotten back in the car than he had to take a piss.

I stopped alongside the road, not far from my apartment, and there he stood, brazenly pissing into the wind.

Before he could stuff it back into his pants, I grabbed his fat dick and went to town with it.

When I say it was fat, I'm not kidding. It wasn't all that long — six inches, at best — but brother, I could barely hold on to that beast with my short little fingers.

It was fat and uncut, just the way I like them. I played with the loose skin, kneading it between my thumb and forefinger, taking folds of it between my teeth and sucking gently.

The coffee must have been doing the trick, because in three minutes flat, he was rock hard.

Standing there in the alley, with our flies unzipped and our cocks blowing in the breeze, we looked amazingly alike. Funny, I wonder if he'd even have given me a second glance if we'd met at a cocktail party.

I dropped to my knees and cupped my hands around his fat dick. My breath was hot and steamy, and I breathed on his meat to get the blood really flowing.

His huge balls completely filled my palms, warming up my fingers. Even in that cold, we were both sweating profusely. I caressed his nut sac with my lips, taking one and then both balls into my mouth, rolling them over my teeth, and tangling the hairs with my spit.

Meanwhile, he was ramming the back of my throat with his brute member. He fucked my mouth wildly, and whenever he showed signs of slowing, I grabbed his ass cheeks with my fingers and pulled him into me again.

Bucking like a bronco, he grabbed my face and plunged into me in one last time before he shot his wad down my gullet.

The hot liquid tasted better than a hot toddy. I licked him dry and tucked his cock back into his pants, zipped up his fly, and patted him on the back as he made his way to the car.

Spent, exhausted, and cold — but sober — we made a beeline for my place, where I made some eggnog and we started up all over again. This time, however, it was the safe way — in bed.

Striking the Pose

When I was eighteen years old, I got into nude modeling. Ever since I was a kid, people had told me what a looker I was, so I figured, *What the hell!*

My hair was almost jet black then; now it's a little gray around the edges. And it hung clear past my shoulders too. When I look at pictures, it's kind of embarrassing. But I'll tell you what: I was quite handsome by the standards of the day. My body back then was tight as a drum too. Though the slim look was in when I was younger, I still had great definition from working out with my older brother's weight set in the garage. It was definitely not hip for us hippies to do that kind of stuff, so I did it kind of on the sly.

But the one thing that hasn't changed in all these years is my cock. Plain and simple, it's a beauty. It hangs about five inches when it's completely soft. When it's stiff, forget about it. I never could find a girl who could take the damn thing, but the guys — they were another story. There was always a buddy here or there who was in the mood for a good piece of dick.

Back then I'd hang out at the beach. That's where I met an agent. He said I could make a lot of dough, and even though material things weren't supposed to mean a lot, we still needed cash to fill our cars and our bellies. My friends thought it would be cool, so I went with this guy back to his office.

170

His office turned out to be a photo studio. Covering the walls were blown-up black-and-white photos of muscle men — all nude. Now, I hadn't known this guy wanted me to shuck my pants, and I was a little nervous. But after a couple of beers, I calmed down enough to at least strip down to my boxers.

This is where my education began. He said he wanted to get some shots of me in a natural state. I wanted to keep my shorts on, so we struck a compromise: The first roll would be with my dick covered up, but it had to be hard. He wanted to see it poking up through my shorts, he said.

Then, since he was the agent and the photographer, he apparently figured it was his job to take care of it. So he strolled right over and planted his big fat hand right on my basket. He started massaging it through the fabric, making it grow longer and thicker with each passing of his fingers.

By then I was rock hard and aching to shoot my wad. With each stroke of his hand and each swig of beer, I was becoming less and less inhibited. But no, he said, I had to wait.

He shot a few pictures of me with my big old cock making a tent of my shorts. Then he said he wanted me naked.

By now, Christ, I couldn't wait to shuck those shorts. As soon as I did, my meat sprang up and poked straight at the ceiling.

He told me I was a natural and shot a few more photos of me in some pretty wild poses.

Then he said that he wanted me soft again, but that was easier said than done. First I had this load to get rid of.

So, casual as all hell, he stepped right over and took my huge tool right in his mouth. He lipped the ridge softly, slipping his stiff tongue into my piss slit.

Then, in one agonizingly slow motion, he took my whole dick into his hot, wet mouth.

He jammed my fuck tool back into his throat, taking all of me with no problem. God, it felt so good for someone to finally take my whole cock. I held him by his shoulders and started swaying back and forth, really getting into it.

jack hart

He didn't slow the pace either. He just kept devouring my cock, slurping on it and chewing on the fat head. He made it stand taller and prouder than I'd ever gotten it.

He was having such a great time, I decided to get in on the action myself. Swinging him around on the floor, I dived onto his basket and unzipped his fly with my teeth. The cold cement floor pressed against our bodies as we sucked each other in a sixty-nine position. I took his limp cock quickly, making it stiff in just under two minutes.

Pumping in unison, we ate each other with a fury, trying to see who could bring the other off first. Sixty-nine is something I don't do often because it's hard to concentrate on what you're getting and what you're giving at the same time.

But this guy was great. He was so appreciative of my giving him head that he moaned his thanks right up my cock, sending shivers throughout my body. He bucked his hips upward as I shoved mine down, and then we both shot off in a torrent of hot, rich juice.

After we cleaned up, he shot a few more pictures of me jerking off. Then I shot a few of him.

It was a great afternoon.

Just last week, as I was cleaning out my garage, I found those photos. And I'll tell you what: They stirred a lot more than old memories.

Video Stars

My friends say I'm something of a dinosaur — that I'm still living in the Dark Ages. Well, maybe that used to be true. I mean, my car is pre-1970, I don't own anything designer, and I hate terra-cotta. I didn't even own a VCR until a few months ago. And you know what? My friends were right: It changed my life.

I really went to town the first month after I got that VCR. I joined three different video clubs just so I wouldn't look like a steady customer in any one of them. I mean, you see a guy renting a couple of fuck films every three weeks or so, and you think nothing of it. Right?

My evenings were filled with nonstop dick and buckets of come. Those X-rated tapes filled my living room with close-ups of one luscious cock after another, close up enough for me to see right down the piss slit.

Seeing dick is great, mind you. But when that's all you're getting, well, it's kind of rough on the groin, you know?

It was then, after I started getting really tired of jacking off alone, that I first noticed Rob. He was the clerk at one of the video stores. The selection at that outlet sucked, and within three short months I'd gone through the entire adult section with no problem. But after a closer look at Rob, I decided to peruse it all over again.

jack hart

He was a short, stocky redhead. His thighs were like tree trunks, and I wondered when in hell he had the time to work out. He was in the store all the time. His wavy, thick hair was cut short. I liked it; it made him look like a lifeguard.

His body was well-defined all over, especially his chest. The way he wore his tank tops drove me right over the edge, especially when I caught a glimpse of his cute little tits.

I could see that he had a hell of a basket under his Jockeys. And his tight butt took up whatever extra fabric was left over from the front of his pants.

After a while we began getting into conversations about the films. At first I would just ask his opinion on this or that, wondering which would be a good buy. And he always gave me straight advice.

I have to admit, though, walking out of there without attracting attention after one of our talks got to be kind of difficult. I found it harder and harder to hide my stiff prick.

Then one day, when I was feeling randy as a rabbit, I decided to take a stroll down to the video store. Rob was there at the counter as usual, as if he had been waiting for me.

No sooner had I walked through the door than he dived under the counter and emerged with a little black cassette case.

"What's that?" I asked, my cock beginning to awaken.

"Check it out."

"A biker film?"

"You got it! I saved a copy just for you. It wasn't easy, man. The other dozen went like hotcakes as soon as I put the poster up in the window."

"Hey, thanks a lot." I grabbed the case, and as I started to walk out the door, a brilliant idea occurred to me.

"So, Rob," I said, turning to face him. "How is it?"

He grinned. "Haven't seen it yet."

"Well, would you like…I mean, what if it's a dud?"

"Tell you what, Brian," he said. "Let's check it out here. That way, if you don't like it, you don't have to pay for it."

174

"Good enough," I said.

We both retreated to the back room where the rental VCRs are repaired. Rob ran out into the store and locked up, putting the OUT TO LUNCH sign in the window. He was whistling happily as he drew back the blue velvet curtain and stepped into the darkness with me.

"Here," he said. He took the tape from my sweaty hands and popped it into the slot. Turning the TV on, we were bathed in the light of the blue snow on-screen. Then the trumpets blared, and a giant penis appeared.

HOT ROD PRODUCTIONS flashed across the TV screen, and a few minutes later a hot-looking dude was stripping before my eyes. There was only one chair, so Rob and I took a seat on the floor, straining to see the TV, which was above our normal field of vision.

It didn't take long for the action to start. Before I knew it, the screen was a mass of naked butts and throbbing dicks, occasionally covered in thick, white juice. It was definitely worth the three dollars.

"Not a bad way to spend the night, huh?" I joked. My cock was aching so badly, I thought I'd die. There was no way on God's green earth that Rob wasn't getting hot too.

In the darkness I reached over and groped his steamy crotch. It was bulging at the seams, the precome already oozing through the denim of his jeans. We didn't say a word as we took to each other like fish to water.

We both stripped silently and quickly and then lay down beside each other on the floor. Very gently Rob began to stroke my body with his fingertips. He started just above my knee (as far down as he could reach), lightly grazing my side up to the nape of my neck. Our cocks stood at attention, head-to-head, barely touching. His body was beautiful in the blue light of the television, and I admired his coppery pubes.

I closed my eyes, savoring the sensations that were shooting through my nerve endings. His fingers glided over every curve and contour of my body, and on the downstroke he brushed my cock — enough to make me want more but not enough to make me shoot. He definitely knew what he was doing.

In an attempt to reciprocate, I let my hand fall to his hip. My fingers massaged his firm ass, gripping a mound of flesh. As I pulled tighter, he moaned and leaned into me enough for my fingertips to reach his ass crack.

They slid in quickly and deftly, and soon I was feeling the moist interior of his ass while he bucked and moaned in rhythm with my caresses. Silently I rose and crawled onto his back, forcing him down, face first, on the plush rug. My rod was slick as spit already, and all I needed to do was point it in the right direction.

I found his hole by nudging at it with my cock head, which popped in easily. He lifted his hips off the floor slightly to accommodate all nine inches of my cock. We moved as one, much like the porn stars on the screen, except that there was a lot less "acting" going on in our session. Everything was perfect; every sound, every sensation, every movement seemed almost choreographed. It was a fantasy, and I hated to utter a single sound for fear that fantasy would burst and I'd awaken in a wet bed once again.

I kissed his neck and nibbled his ear as I fucked him from behind. He softly murmured nasty suggestions, and I had to strain to pick them up. When I did, they just got me hotter.

Then Rob started to rock back and forth to silent music. Soon we were lying on our sides like spoons in a drawer. I reached around his hips once again and took hold of his dripping dick. I matched my every forward thrust with a stroke on his rod. He closed his eyes, imagining that he was fucking my ass. So we lay there, fucking each other in our dreams.

But even dreams come to an end, and our climax came quietly, slowly — no splashy fireworks, just complete surrender. It was nothing like that shit I'd been watching on the screen. I thought I might be in love with him.

After that, though, I saw him only now and then. We never needed another film to get us up, but we'd watch one occasionally just to remember that sweaty afternoon on the floor in the back room of the video store.

Travel Advisory

When I stepped through the metal detector at the airport, I set off the alarm. The expressionless young woman in the guard's uniform had me empty my pockets of my car keys and a handful of change. The alarm rang as I stepped through a second time. Then I took off my watch and my ID bracelet. Again, a ringing. Still maintaining a casual attitude about the whole episode, she ran a handheld metal detector over my body: up my sides, out along my arms, then down along my legs. When it reached my crotch, it began making a really embarrassing whooping noise. *Oh, shit!* I thought, finally remembering.

She looked more alert this time and called a male guard over. He was a head taller than I am, and he had dark, serious eyes and a full black mustache, which turned down menacingly at the corners. From the open collar of his blue shirt spilled tufts of wiry black hair.

"It's just down there," the woman said, pointing the metal detector at my crotch again. The annoying whooping sound started again as she pointed.

The male guard gestured for me to follow him, and we proceeded into a small room with a window looking out onto the runway. That would be my plane out there, where luggage was being loaded into the cargo hold.

178

"I'll have to ask you to drop your trousers, sir," he said, his gruff tone clashing with his polite words. This guy was clearly in charge, and he knew it and expected me to know it too.

Feeling more embarrassed by the second but not knowing what to say, I unzipped and lowered my faded blue jeans. The guard aimed his metal detector at the bulge in my briefs. It whooped for a few seconds before he waved it away.

"The undershorts will have to come down too," he said, looking grim, his dark eyes unreadable.

I wanted the floor to swallow me up. I was mortified to within an inch of my life, but I knew I had to comply with his request, so I pulled my underpants down to my knees. My cock was soft but fully extended. I've always been proud of its size and the way it plumps out in the middle whenever something catches its interest.

I thought I saw the guard's eyebrows shoot up when he saw the metal-studded leather band encircling my cock and balls.

"What's that?" he asked, looking at my crotch with widening eyes. His irises, I realized, were not dark but tawny, sort of like a police dog's, in fact. They had that same fearlessness and suggestion of authority. His face, though tanned to a shade of light walnut, showed the blue shadow of a beard beneath the skin of his jaw.

I hesitated and then said, "It's a cock ring." My roommate had slipped it on me that morning as a bon voyage gift, saying it would bring me luck. I had completely forgotten that I was wearing it.

The guard's lips were parted slightly as he stared at it. He put the metal detector back in its holster. It seemed his cheeks were beginning to redden; I know my cock was getting hard.

He lifted his right hand slightly, palm up, as though he had a notion of taking hold of my cock. But he made no move toward me. With my heart pounding, I stepped toward him. The head of my cock touched his warm, dry fingers, which then slid along the underside of my shaft to cup my balls. He could've had me

179

singing soprano if he'd wanted, but his grip, though firm and a little scary, didn't squeeze. Instead it made me feel warm and submissive. I glanced out the window and saw passengers boarding the plane. I was on the verge of being willing to miss my flight.

"You've got time," he murmured in a low voice. Still holding me, he took his left hand and unzipped his pants, pulling the pouch of a blue bikini to one side. A big, thick uncut dick flopped out of his fly, surrounded at the base by a thatch of black hair. He reached in and pulled out his big balls, which were swirled with black hair. I could smell his essence.

With both hands he held our cocks together, the top of mine against the underside of his, and slowly pumped them. His cock, now fully rigid, was quite meaty.

Outside on the tarmac the loading continued. Inside that room I felt myself descending into the slide toward inevitable orgasm, and I pressed my face against the mass of chest hair peeking out from his shirt collar. He was feeling it too; I could sense the tension mounting in his big body.

He pulled a handkerchief out of his hip pocket and wrapped it around my dick head, gripping our two cocks more tightly and pumping more erratically. We were both very close.

I quickly pulled out my own handkerchief and wrapped it in two layers around his mushroom-shaped cock head. I was ready when I felt his cock start to jump. My load shot up through my shaft, and I jerked against his hand as I spurted. His body shuddered, and I felt the handkerchief going wet against my palm. His chin was against my shoulder, his cheek against my cheek. I smelled a spicy aftershave over a sexy, masculine scent.

He straightened up and tucked the handkerchief, now soaked with my come, into his breast pocket. Then, without saying a single word or even looking at me, he zipped himself up and strode out of the room.

I put my own handkerchief, sloppy with his come, in my carry-on bag, pulled up my shorts and jeans, and scurried down the hall to the gate. All the other passengers had boarded the plane by now. At the top of the boarding stairs, I turned to look back at the terminal. I saw the guard looking out a window toward the plane. He didn't wave; he just held his bunched-up handkerchief to his nose.

Indian Summer

It was late fall, the leaves were turning, and the air was chilly — but not today. It was Indian summer and very warm, almost eighty degrees. Paul and I were playing basketball at the playground a block away from his house, which is what we did a lot — almost too much. I spent way too much time across town with Paul, and sometimes it made my dad a little mad. But he wasn't home very much because of his job, and he was glad I had someplace safe to go instead of staying home alone and being bored.

Today seemed different somehow, but I couldn't put my finger on it. We were done shooting baskets, and both of us had to piss really bad, so we were hurrying down the street to Paul's house, almost running. Reaching the front door first (I always could outrun him), I was down the hall when I realized that we hadn't agreed who would go first. I turned to say something, but Paul knew what I was thinking. "I can't wait," he said. "We'll go together, like the trough at the drive-in." I couldn't wait either, so in we went. We each pulled a leg of our gym shorts up and our jocks back, and both started to go. Then I looked over and saw something I had never seen before — Paul's dick, and it was uncut. In the eight months I had known him, I had never seen him naked. Even when I stayed all night, he always had shorts or something on.

I had seen other guys before at school (I was nineteen and still in high school because I'd flunked a grade when Mom and Dad divorced), but none of them was uncut, so it was interesting to look at, and it was just a little bigger than mine. I must have been staring at it because he put it away fast and turned to leave. Suddenly he turned back and said, "You know what? Your shorts and shirt are soaked with sweat, and it's getting dark and cold, and you're going to freeze on the bus going home. Why don't we take a shower, and I'll loan you some dry clothes to wear home." That made sense to me. Then he said his water heater was going out and there might not be enough hot water for both of us, so we should take a shower together. I hesitated, but Paul said, "Don't worry, just pretend you're in gym class." I thought for a minute, then said okay. Paul reached into the tub enclosure and turned on the water, then started to get undressed.

I had just finished removing my shoes and socks, but Paul was already down to his jock. He looked over and said, "Hurry before the water runs out." Then he said, "Here," and reached over and grabbed my T-shirt, pulling it off. I pulled my shorts and jock off, and Paul said, "Go on, get in," so I did. Then he stepped in and slid the door closed. Even though I had taken showers here before, the tub seemed smaller.

I was snapped back to reality when Paul reached over my shoulder to douse the washcloth. He let his elbows rest on my shoulders, which brought him very close to me. I noticed that it felt strange but good to have him that close. "Hand me the soap," he said. I turned, picked it up, and watched as he soaped the rag. Then he said, "Give me your hand." I reached up with my right hand. He took it and started to wash my arm. I wasn't sure what to do, but it felt good, so I just stood there. He swiped the cloth up one arm and down the other, then around my neck and down my chest and belly to my belt line. The rag was a little coarse, but his gentle touch made it feel so good that I didn't want him to stop. "Turn around," he said. Then he washed my shoulders and back, but he didn't stop at the waist this time. He skipped my butt and started down one leg and up the other, reaching around to get to the front.

Then I felt the washcloth on my butt, its coarseness tingling my skin. I felt my asshole tighten up, and my head fell back as I moaned, "Oh, God, that feels good!" Then I felt the rag push between my cheeks, moving up and down till it found my pucker, gently rubbing against it. My whole body tensed up, and I moaned again. I had never felt anything like it. It was fantastic, and I never wanted it to stop.

I started to hear voices. It was Paul. "Turn around," he was saying. When I did he said, "Well, look here." When I looked I saw the biggest hard-on I had ever had. It was so hard, it hurt. Then he took the rag and ran it over my crotch and balls. I begged him to rub my butt some more. "In a minute," he said, adding, "Want to feel even better?"

"Yes," I said, though I couldn't imagine anything better than that rag on my ass.

As I looked down, Paul reached out with his tongue and licked the underside of my cock. My head reeled, then I felt his lips slowly sliding over the head and down the shaft while his tongue was still lapping the head. I grabbed the door and wall so I wouldn't fall down. His head went back and forth several times, and then the world was set on fire. I felt two rags — one rubbing my butt, the other slowly crawling up the crack from my crotch and doing circles around my asshole.

It was even better than before. My body began to convulse. I couldn't catch my breath. My dick was so hard, I thought it would explode — and then it did! I started shooting wave after wave, my juice pushing up from my balls and running up my dick so forcefully that I thought it would blow the head clean off. I heard Paul choking and managed to look down. Paul was desperately trying to keep up, but he couldn't. My come was running — almost shooting — out of his mouth. When I finally stopped, I was so weak that Paul had to catch me and help me sit down. I then watched him as he jacked himself to a noisy climax. Then he gently rinsed me off, washing his come off me, and helped me to bed. Needless to say, I spent that night and many more in his arms. And, yes, that rag still feels good on my ass, and so does he.

The Self-portrait

The summer before I left home to go to college, I fixed up a bedroom in the basement of my parents' house so I could have more privacy, away from the prying eyes of my little brother. Of course, I was as horny as an eighteen-year-old could ever hope to be, and I remember that summer as an endless round of jacking off. I would beat off two, three, even four times a day, always shooting big, messy loads that required a lot of cleaning up. Since the bathrooms were both upstairs, this necessitated some planning on my part. I was always determined to eat my own load, but somehow, as soon as I came, I would lose the gumption — or should I say appetite? — and opt for the more traditional modes of cleaning myself up.

I had a Polaroid camera, and ever since I'd found some hardcore porn snapshots in my father's desk a few months earlier — apparently he was as oversexed as I was (and still am!) — I was fascinated by the idea of photos showing hard-ons and come shots and stuff like that. My father's porn photos were of men fucking women, I was disappointed to note, but I still managed to come several times whenever I looked at those little black-and-white pictures he'd hidden away.

Anyway, one day I was looking for a new thrill, something to spice up my masturbatory revels, and I hit upon the idea of taking pictures of myself jacking off. After some experimenting I figured out how to get a good shot with my Polaroid by aiming the camera at a mirror showing my reflection. If I shot the picture from an angle, the flash wouldn't show in the mirror, and since I was interested in pictures that showed only my boner, I didn't worry about the camera's blocking my face.

With my white cotton briefs pushed down around my ankles (I've always gotten into that look), I sat my naked ass on a stool in front of my full-length mirror and put on a Doors album. Just the thought of Jim Morrison's sexy lips always made me hard as a rock. I slathered on some of my favorite lube and started stroking my meat, which soon reached its fairly respectable measure of seven and a half thick uncut inches. I got into it more than I would have guessed, lewdly stretching my foreskin out as wide as it would go, then getting a good shot of it with the head of my dick peeking out, kind of like a pink turtle. It wasn't long before I was spewing a steady stream of precome. Man! Having the camera trained on my own crotch was an unbelievable turn-on for me.

After I had used up most of the exposures — all variously obscene views of my greased-up prick — I was growing impatient with myself and wanted to come. I once again felt the urge to eat my load, so I lay down on the floor in front of the mirror and, after much tinkering around, devised a way to prop the camera up within reach so I could hit the shutter at the crucial moment. I threw my legs up in the air over my head and pointed my dick at my mouth as I started stroking in earnest. Jim Morrison was crooning "The End," and for some reason the part about killing his father and fucking his mother made me blow my wad. It took a lot of control on my part, but I managed to trip the shutter of my camera just as a long streamer of jizz flew out of my cock in the general direction of my gaping mouth. Naturally, I was jerking around so wildly that only a tiny bit of my load landed on my tongue. The rest, to my dismay, went up my nose, on my hair, and in my eyes. And everybody knows it burns like hell to get come in your eyes.

jack hart

I needed running water — and fast. Stifling a whimper of pain, I hurried out of my room with my underpants still hobbling my ankles. But my desire to see the come shot I'd just taken outweighed my sense of logic, so I grabbed the still-developing photo in one greasy hand as I headed for the laundry room and the sink that was there.

Imagine my horror as I lunged through the laundry-room door and found my father standing there, flipping through his latest issue of *Hustler.* He was engrossed in his own porn, so I don't really think he was fully aware of the state his son was in, but I fucking flipped out! I did an immediate about-face — no mean feat with a pair of Towncraft briefs twisted around my ankles — and raced back to the sanctuary of my bedroom. Flustered beyond belief and freaked out to the point of idiocy, I tripped in the doorway and did a belly flop right on the floor, landing halfway inside my room and halfway out. The force of my crash landing made me drop my latest self-portrait, but I wasn't thinking about that. No, I was concerned only with crawling like some big white slug back into my makeshift photo studio and locking the door behind me.

Only when I was safely behind my bedroom door did the mortifying realization wash over me that the come shot was on the floor out in the basement hall. I was about to attempt a rescue when I heard my father come thumping toward my door. Evidently my crazed-bull impersonation had caused him to abandon his skin mag so he could investigate the ruckus. With my heart seemingly pounding ice water through my veins — never again have I felt so cold — I heard my father bark my name and rap sharply on my door. Knowing I was trapped, I meekly opened my door a crack and timidly peered out. He thrust his big paw through the opening and waved the incriminating photo in my face. "This yours?" he asked. I nodded numbly. "Nice shot," he commented dryly. "But for Christ's sake, don't leave things like that lying around. Your mother would flip her fuckin' lid."

HEAT

I watched in speechless amazement as he turned on his heel and ambled off down the hall. After that we seemed to get along better than we ever had before.

Night Moves

During the middle of the night, I woke up with a raging hard-on. Ordinarily, I would have thrown the covers back and taken matters into my own hand. But this night I couldn't: My new roommate, Oscar, was sound asleep next to me. Oscar was from Venezuela. He was tall — six feet two — and well-built. When I first looked into his deep brown eyes, I thought my cock would rip a hole in my jeans. However, Oscar was rabidly heterosexual. Whenever I mentioned gays — even just in passing — he made his contempt clear.

Knowing he wouldn't be pleased to wake up and find me jacking off, I rolled over and tried to go back to sleep. But the throbbing between my legs got only worse. With a sigh I rolled onto my back. Then I reached down and pulled open the leg hole of my briefs. With a little encouragement, my stiff tool and balls sprang free. With my left hand I positioned my cock below my left thigh so that the top was touching my thigh and the underside was accessible to my fingers. Gently I stroked its length. I licked my fingers and massaged the spit into the sensitive region where cock head meets cock belly. The effect was quite stimulating, and I felt my cock stiffen further. Several times I had to lick my fingers because the spit dried on my steamy rod. But soon I was producing enough sticky precome to lubricate my rapidly moving digits.

190

Just then, Oscar rolled over to face me. I froze. My muscles started aching from the tension, but I dared not move. I thought for sure that my rustling about had disturbed him, but he seemed to still be sleeping. He muttered his American girlfriend's name and then resumed his rhythmic breathing. I could feel his hot breath on my shoulder. That alone was almost enough to set me off in my horny state, but I fought back the temptation to quickly get my rocks off.

If I hadn't been so horny, I never would have had the guts to do it, but I reached out with my right hand — as if moving in my sleep — and let my palm nestle against Oscar's groin. His pecker was quite soft, though of impressive dimensions. His balls were almost hot to the touch. Moving very slowly, I slipped my fingers into the leg opening of his briefs. I had to stretch the elastic only a few inches before I felt his nuts brush past my fingers on their way to freedom.

By now I was trembling. I knew that if he caught me, Oscar would beat the hell out of me. Emboldened by the thickness between my own legs, I scooped up his balls. My hand was barely big enough to hold both of them. It was a warm night, and they hung loose in their sac, which was coated with sweat. I took my time rolling them around in my hand. After a few minutes my hand was covered in his sweat. I brought my right hand up to my nose while fondling my own cock with my left. The manly ball scent made my head spin. I could have spilled my nuts just from sniffing his musk.

I again reached for his balls. As my fingers worked their way up the base of Oscar's cock, I was surprised to find it quite stiff. Evidently Oscar enjoyed being manhandled in his sleep, even if he thought he wouldn't like it when he was awake. I was surprised to find that his dick had risen right out the top of his shorts and was extending another four or five inches beyond. It was hot and hard.

With my dick now awash in precome from my pulling on it with my left hand, I covered the fingertips of my right hand with the sticky stuff. Then I wrapped my fingers around Oscar's cock head and smeared the cock juice over the rim with a motion similar to screwing a lid on a jar. After a few twists his rod stiffened considerably. Encouraged, I transferred more lubricant. It took several trips to completely cover the head. I began a gentle twisting motion over the engorged cock head. I could feel his cock start to twitch and squirm in my hand. I had to milk my cock for more lubricant as Oscar's hot flesh absorbed it. But soon precome was oozing from Oscar's piss hole. Quickly the flow became heavy enough to start running between my fingers. Oscar's breathing was much heavier as his hips began a slow thrusting motion in my direction. He called out his girlfriend's name and with a groan started thrusting mightily into my palm. As his excitement grew, I had only to hold my hand steady to provide a tight, slippery tunnel for that plunging cock. I could smell the sweat pearling on Oscar's chest as he neared the peak. The smell, sound, and feel of a healthy male in rut and my own hand working my cock had me on the brink.

Oscar moaned loudly. I had time to turn my hand as I felt his manhood swell. Then four powerful shots filled my cupped hand with warm, slippery man juice. Reluctantly I drew my hand away from Oscar's gusher because I knew that the intensity of his climax would rouse him shortly, revealing me as the party responsible for his "nighttime emission."

Oscar continued to thrash about for perhaps another minute before settling down. "Bob, you awake?" he whispered. Even if I *had* been asleep, I couldn't have slept through all that groaning, but I pretended I was.

Oscar felt around on the bed. I could hear his fingers sliding over the come-drenched sheets. With a little sigh he got up and made his way to the bathroom.

When I saw the light go on underneath the door and heard the water running in the basin, I threw back the covers. Oscar's come was leaking from between the fingers of my cupped hand. Quickly I applied it to my rigid cock. Seconds later my hand was flying over my hard-on. The scent of Oscar's sperm was thick in the air. With a few quick strokes, my long-delayed load shot forth. The hot, spicy liquid rained down on my neck and chest as my hand struggled to control my raging member.

I lay there for just a moment to catch my breath. Then I smeared the sticky fluid over my chest. I lay back without covering up so that the lusty aroma would fill the room. I wanted Oscar to smell what sort of effect he had had on me, even if I could never tell him face-to-face. When I heard the toilet flush, I covered up. As Oscar got back in bed, I rolled over on my side to face him so he would have to smell the fresh come drying on my chest.

Florida or Bust

I travel a good bit and periodically pick up a friendly-looking hitchhiker for company. I sometimes flirt with my passenger but usually let it go at that.

One evening last fall I had been to dinner with my parents in a nearby town and was driving back to my apartment when I saw someone walking up ahead near the drawbridge. He seemed to be of medium height and build and was carrying a small knapsack on his back. He was walking slowly and looked a little sad. I pulled over just ahead of him.

"Where are you going?" I asked, smiling at him.

"Trying to get to Florida," he said, opening the passenger door and getting in. "Wow, it feels good to get out of the heat." I told him that I was going only a few miles but would be glad to get him to the other side of town or even on the interstate about ten miles away. "That would be great," he said.

As we started into the flow of traffic, I cautiously studied my passenger and found him to be a most attractive young man. "Where are you coming from?" I asked.

"Texas," he said. "I just got out of the service, and I'm going to live with my folks until I get my feet on the ground."

Our small talk continued, and I found that he had a nice smile and beautiful eyes. The bulge at his crotch was also noteworthy. "By the way, my name is Jim," I said, extending my hand.

194

He eagerly took my hand in his own, clasping it firmly. "Hi, my name is Bryan. I'm glad to meet you — and thanks for picking me up back there. I'd been walking for over a mile."

"I'm glad to oblige," I said, and added, "Bryan, may I ask you a personal question?"

He shrugged his shoulders and said, "Sure."

I took a deep breath. "I don't mean to offend you, but I would like to know — do you like to get sucked?"

There was a long silence, perhaps a minute, before he spoke. "Are you gay?" he asked.

"Yes, I am," I replied, "but that's no reflection on you. I only asked if you liked to get sucked."

There was another period of silence, and then he chuckled softly. "I don't understand. I think you want to suck my dick, but what would you get out of it?"

It was my turn to chuckle. "If you did understand, you would be gay," I replied. "I'll be very gentle. All you have to do is relax and enjoy."

There was another period of silence, and we saw the sign indicating our approach to the highway. "If I let you do it," he said with misgiving in his voice, "could I sleep on your couch? I'm really tired."

I smiled at him and joked, "In the words of Conrad Hilton, Be my guest!"

We got to my apartment, and I ushered him inside, showed him the bathroom, and laid out fresh towels and soap. As he cleaned the dirt from his body, I tidied up a bit and put on some music. Bryan emerged from the bathroom fresh and clean and smiling, his black wavy hair still damp. "That hot shower was wonderful," he said. "I feel like my old self again." I motioned to a comfortable chair for him to sit in and got him a beer and myself a glass of wine. He told me about his two years of military service right out of high school. As he finished his beer, I noticed some hesitancy in his voice and in his manner.

"You have nothing to fear from me," I assured him.

"I know," he said and smiled at me. "I've just never done this before — I don't know what to expect."

"Just relax," I said.

I led him to my bedroom and indicated the edge of the bed, where I wanted him to sit and lie back. As he removed the bathrobe I had provided for him, I marveled at his physical beauty. He had olive skin and an abundance of black body hair, especially on his legs and chest, which was surprisingly well-muscled. He was perhaps five foot six or seven. I turned off the light to make him feel more at ease and said, "Just relax." I knelt between his legs.

He was flaccid, but that was to be expected. I placed his member in my mouth and sucked, lightly licking under the head on that very sensitive spot of flesh. Bryan moaned, shifted his weight, and slid a little closer to me. I stopped and asked, "Are you all right?"

He heaved a big sigh and said, "Oh, yes."

I continued gently sucking on his penis, which within another minute was completely erect and most impressive, perhaps seven inches long and very thick. I took great care in sucking that young man's dick, being very deliberate, moving my lips slowly up and down his shaft.

Bryan was very responsive, replying to my ministrations with moans and gentle movements of his body. He put his hands on my shoulders, fondled my neck, and ran his fingers through my hair. "Oh, stop! Stop!" he said, and I did as instructed. He lay there on the verge of orgasm, and I moved back a bit, massaging his calves, feeling the sexy hair between my fingers. "I haven't had sex in several weeks," he said matter-of-factly. "I'm afraid I'm going to come real soon," he added, a note of anxiety in his voice.

"It's okay," I assured him. "That's the whole point." After he settled down a bit, I returned to the task before me, slowly sucking his erect penis. I savored the fresh, clean scent of him and the taste of his dick, which had enjoyed only women before

196

now. I could tell he was getting close to the edge because he tensed and was breathing hard.

"Here it comes," he whispered shudderingly as the onslaught of orgasm washed over him.

I kept the head of his dick in my mouth and continued licking beneath the cock head as the copious flow of semen filled my mouth. I swallowed gratefully, then nursed his penis tenderly and lovingly, not wishing to miss a single drop. At last I released him, sat back, and asked, "Are you okay?"

He laughed. "That was certainly different. I can't say that this is something I want to do again, but it was pretty wild." He sat up and put his hands on my shoulders and gently shook me. "You really know what you're doing."

I replied, "You fairly inspired me." We both laughed, and when we stood up, I asked, "I know you're straight, and I'm not asking for anything in return, but could I hug you?" Without any hesitation he put his arms around me and held me close. I enfolded him, and we held each other for several minutes. I kissed the top of his head and the side of his clean-shaven face.

"I still don't know what you got out of this," he said.

"More satisfaction than I've have in months," I said. *Plus a marvelous opportunity to work on my oral fixation,* I thought to myself, but I didn't say it.

True to my word, I fixed him a bed on the sofa, and he slept soundly until I had to rouse him the next morning. Bryan was a little shy as I drove him to the freeway, but when I stopped to let him out, he leaned toward me and gently kissed me on the lips. The sweetness and tenderness in this young man touched me profoundly. He said quite simply, "Thanks." He waved and walked away, leaving me with a beatific smile on my face.

Anatomy 101

"**H**i," I finally said to him one day after watching his every move in our evening photography class for over a month.

"Hello," he replied with a sly smile, his attentive hazel eyes gazing directly into my gray ones. He sat down at the desk next to me, then glanced surreptitiously at my face, waiting to see my reaction. I stared shyly down at my notes, hoping he couldn't see my trembling hands or hear the heavy pounding of my heart. I smelled the faint but pleasant scent of his cologne as he leaned over toward me. "Are you enjoying this class so far?" he inquired.

I nodded. As I turned my head to look at him fully, I noticed that he was as gorgeous close-up as he was from afar. He was Mediterranean, I decided. Along with those beautiful eyes, he had soft-looking coffee-colored hair cut short and a sensual smile that would knock any levelheaded gay man off his feet.

"I'm Eric," I finally managed to say.

"Nice to meet you, Eric. I'm Nathaniel. Nathan for short." He took my small hand in his considerably larger warm one and shook it. Then class began. As the professor lectured us, I studied Nathan's profile. More than once, his eyes met mine.

After class I stood up, and Nathan jumped quickly to his feet, helping me into my coat.

"That was a very interesting class, don't you think?" he murmured to me from behind. The intimate tone of his voice made me want him more than ever.

"Yes, very interesting. I'm really beginning to love photography," I replied inanely as we walked out of the classroom together. "I just wish I had more equipment at home to work with. The machines here are always busy."

"Would you like to come up to my apartment and see my equipment? My photography equipment, that is!" Nathan chuckled. "I just got a new enlarger."

I accepted his offer, feeling a twinge of delight in my stomach. We strolled to his cozy apartment four blocks away.

In the elevator things began to heat up. I suddenly felt his strong arms come around me from behind and his soft lips caress my neck with sweet passion. I turned around, still in his arms, and met his lips with mine. Our tongues touched briefly, then tangled together as if in battle. The elevator door opened abruptly, and to my surprise, Nathan lifted me up and carried me into his apartment, still kissing me feverishly.

"I want you," he said breathlessly. "I want to make love to you, Eric." He broke contact with me suddenly as if waiting for my response. With trembling hands I began to undress. I got as far as my shirt when Nathan stepped in to assist. He didn't touch my chest but ran his strong hands smoothly over my back. I felt almost too exposed as he stared at my bare torso, touching my nipples with his eyes but not his hands.

"Do you like what you see?" I asked, smiling.

"They're beautiful," Nathan murmured, smiling back at me.

Mesmerized by his eyes and hypnotized by his soft voice, I let him unzip my pants. I stepped out of them and stood naked before him. Nathan ran his hands over my buttocks. I responded by lying back on his sofa and beckoning him to me. He lay gently on top of me, and I wrapped my legs around him tightly. The throbbing bulge under his jeans told me he wanted me, and I was as eager as he. I smiled as Nathan gazed intently at my entire body, now completely naked. His eyes took in every feature of my anatomy, including my slightly spread legs.

"You're so beautiful," he whispered, "even more than I ever imagined."

I sat up on the sofa and undid his pants, pulling them down slowly. By now Nathan was visibly excited. I ripped the rest of his clothes off, wanting him more and more as I saw his muscular physique. He stiffened in my hand as I fondled his balls and cock. I squirmed on the sofa, wanting release but not wanting the sweet tension to the end.

"I want you inside me!" I finally cried out, and Nathan obediently shoved three fingers inside my ass, pushing them in and retreating faster as I groaned with pleasure. I then felt the delicate sensation of his tongue on my erect penis. This was more than I could bear, and I climaxed, the spasms exploding through my lower body while I moaned in ecstasy.

I opened my eyes. Nathan was leaning over me, brushing a loose strand of hair from my face. I rolled over onto my stomach. I could feel his body over me; his hard cock pulsated just outside my damp opening. I spread my legs again, letting him inside me. As he thrust his hardened shaft into my ass again and again, we seemingly meshed as though we were one. Nathan moaned heavily as his hot liquid spurted inside me.

We both relaxed for a moment, not talking. We must have fallen asleep for a few hours; I awoke sweaty and satisfied. Nathan opened his eyes soon after.

Nathan sighed, picked me up in those strong arms, and carried me to the bathroom, nuzzling me as he turned on the shower, still holding me tight.

"I'm glad I got this chance to make use of your, ah, enlarger," I whispered, smiling, and Nathan laughed.

Heat Wave

It was late August, and the heat was almost unbearable. The entire city was in a pissy mood because of the intense heat, and I was no exception. I'd been stuck in traffic for an hour after a particularly stressful day at work. All I wanted to do was to get into my cool apartment and unwind. Actually, there was one other thing I wanted to do, and that was to dump the load that had been building up in my balls for the past three days. I wanted release — bad.

After I finally got home, I walked up the two flights of stairs to my apartment, where I knew my lover would be asleep. He worked crazy hours, so he slept at odd intervals throughout the day. Not wanting to disturb him, I quietly went in and set my briefcase on the kitchen table. There was a little drawing taped to the saltshaker of a naked man holding a kitten. I smiled at Jeff's work and went into the john. A nagging pressure in my crotch had been bothering me all day, and it wasn't all from a pent-up bladder.

I sighed audibly as the flow started. The sensation of relief was overwhelming. I shook my cock dry and stuffed it back in my pants. I stepped over to the mirror and removed my tie, then my shirt, and laid them on top of the hamper. Jeff would wash them for me. As I looked at myself, I planned how I would get off. My every thought was directed toward masturbating. Since

jack hart

I don't cruise anymore and Jeff gets bitchy if I wake him up too early, I've been doing a lot of that lately.

My fly was being tented by my most prized possession. I unsnapped and zipped down. The little tent was still there, but now it was formed by my boxers. A dark spot appeared where precome oozed out of my little buddy's mouth like a perverted drool. Man, if those shorts could talk!

I smiled wistfully as I hooked my finger under the elastic band of those tattletale shorts and pushed them below my knees. When I bent over to work them off my feet, my ass crack smiled wide as the cool air invaded. It felt good on my asshole. One hand shot back there and ran its way along the crack, gently pushing on my man pussy. I wanted to get fucked, but that would have to wait for Jeff and his little buddy — or rather, big buddy. Jeff's dick is nine inches when soft and about ten when hard. He has one of those dicks that get hard but not much bigger. That's perfectly okay since it's big enough for me (and for half the rest of the world).

Now completely naked, I walked to the full-length mirror on the door in the bedroom. My dick happily bounced, rejoicing in the cool air. Jeff was lying faceup on the bed. A sheet clung to him in all the right places and made me even hotter. As always when he slept, he was nude. His smooth chest rose and fell in rhythm with his breathing. His alabaster skin looked almost tan in the dim light. One arm was flung up over his head, and the other rested on his belly just above his patch of wiry black pubic hair. Right below, the sheet hid his massive cock from view.

That was slightly disappointing. I fought the urge to sneak over and pull the sheet away and devour his meat. He needed his rest. His eyes darted about under his closed lids in some dream or another, and I wondered if I was a part of it.

A tugging in my loins called me back to my duty. I had to satisfy my best friend so that he would continue to perform whenever I needed him. I give him regular workouts, and he gives me ropy strands of come and eye-rolling orgasms. It's mutually

202

rewarding. I reluctantly turned away from Jeff to face the mirror once more and gingerly rubbed the underside of my cock with an index finger until my dick swelled to the limit. I moaned softly as the pleasure started to flow. My stroking progressed to a milking motion as I grasped the base and pulled the loose skin up toward the head and then back down after it had been stretched as far as it would go.

The longer I continued, the better it felt. I cupped my balls with my free hand and squeezed while I pushed at the base of my cock from behind. Stroking and squeezing, stroking and squeezing, I continued to work my lust into action. A rivulet of precome oozed out, and I quickly caught it on a finger. I brought it to my mouth and closed my eyes as I tasted the pungent flavor only a man can appreciate.

My ball sac went from loose and dangling to tight and elevated. My stroking continued until I started to feel the tingle of warning that comes right before an orgasm starts. I let go of my cock, and it swung from left to right. I wanted to prolong the pleasure, but it didn't understand. The head was dark red, and the shaft jerked involuntarily every few seconds. A dull ache started to develop somewhere under my pubes, so I knew it was getting close to the time to shoot my spunk. I envisioned the first spurt of hot jism exploding and landing on the mirror. It would slowly slide down and separate into clear and opaque parts as the subsequent blasts hit the glass. Some of it would dribble onto my fingers, and I would lap it up like ambrosia.

The bed creaked. I turned around. Jeff was awake! He smiled, and he must have exposed every tooth in his head. One of those infamous tents rose autonomously in front of him. His mussed hair and hairless chest made him look like a little boy. The look in his eyes was all man, though. My hungry hole might get what it wanted after all.

Dr. Love

I've always been extremely turned on by medical examinations. I just love the clinical atmosphere and the stiff white paper sheets they make you lie on. It all just makes me horny as hell.

One day last month I had an appointment for my yearly physical. I arrived at the office a little early because I had just switched to a new doctor and was eager to experience a new technique. As soon as I entered the lobby, I saw him through the glass partition. I knew I wouldn't be disappointed.

He wasn't really that handsome. Rather, he was bookish-looking and had big round wire-frame eyeglasses and short-cropped hair. It was swept up over his forehead, making him look much older than I guessed he was. If you looked up *doctor* in the dictionary, you'd probably find his picture.

He asked me to strip down to my socks, then left the room. I just got hotter and hotter thinking about everything he was going to do to me! I fought off a growing erection and lay back on the table, my legs spread wide. Just then the doctor came back.

He checked my vital signs. *No need to do that,* I thought, *I know I'm alive!* He quickly worked his way down my abdomen, and I felt a stirring in my cock as his hands brushed the top of my pubic bush. He told me he needed to check my pulse before and after some mild exercise.

I started doing some jumping jacks, my dong slapping my belly with each count. I noticed the doctor staring at my cock as my balls bounced around. I stopped, and he took my pulse again. So far, so good. Brother, he didn't know the half of it!

He slid forward in his chair, cupped my balls, and asked me to cough. I've got really sensitive balls, and I just loved this. I coughed twice, and he removed his hands. My balls pounded with excitement, and I was wishing there had been a problem so we could've run through the test again.

Next he told me to spread my legs wide. "Relax," he said, "this won't hurt a bit." I felt subservient and wildly excited as I watched him lubricate his fingers (over rubber gloves, of course). He pushed his finger into my hole and massaged my insides gently. I could feel the come surging through my balls. My back arched involuntarily, and I gasped. He seemed to be warming his hands by the heat of my asshole. All the hairs from the back of my neck to my pubes stood on end: I felt the onslaught coming, but I consciously suppressed it.

It was a weird feeling: wanting to come and not wanting to come, both at the same time. Actually, wondering if I'd be able to hold it back was proving to be more of a thrill than actually reaching orgasm.

By now my dick was growing at a steady rate, but the sheet kept it hidden from his view.

He pinched and prodded my entire body, looking for some sign of an impending disease. Meanwhile, I stalled by relating every cough and sneeze I'd ever had since I was four years old, and just as I got to the part about my bout with the measles, he reached over and locked the door.

"Maybe you need an internal exam," he grinned.

Got a story to tell with an incredible climax?
Jack Hart is seeking contributions for future
editions in his *Heat* series of true gay sexual
encounters. Submissions should be shorter
than 2,000 words and become the
property of Jack Hart.
Send them to Jack Hart c/o Alyson Books, PO
Box 4371, Los Angeles, CA 90078.

alyson
books

B-BOY BLUES, by James Earl Hardy. A seriously sexy, fiercely funny, black-on-black love story. A walk on the wild side turns into more than Mitchell Crawford ever expected. "A lusty, freewheeling first novel.... Hardy has the makings of a formidable talent." *–Kirkus Reviews*

2ND TIME AROUND, by James Earl Hardy. The sequel to best-seller *B-Boy Blues.* "An upbeat tale that—while confronting issues of violence, racism, and homophobia—is romantic, absolutely sensual, and downright funny." *–Publishers Weekly*

MY BIGGEST O, edited by Jack Hart. What was the best sex you ever had? Jack Hart asked that question of hundreds of gay men, and got some fascinating answers. Here are summaries of the most intriguing of them. Together, they provide an engaging picture of the sexual tastes of gay men.

MY FIRST TIME, edited by Jack Hart. Hart has compiled a fascinating collection of true, first-person stories by men from around the country, describing their first same-sex sexual encounter.

THE DAY WE MET, edited by Jack Hart. Hart presents true stories by gay men who provide intriguing looks at the different origins of their long-term relationships. However love first arose, these stories will be sure to delight, inform, and touch you.

THE PRESIDENT'S SON, by Krandall Kraus. President Marshall's son is gay. The president, who is beginning a tough battle for reelection, knows it but can't handle it. *"The President's Son*...is a delicious, oh-so-thinly veiled tale of a political empire gone insane." *–The Washington Blade*

THE LORD WON'T MIND, by Gordon Merrick. In this first volume of the classic trilogy, Charlie and Peter forge a love that will survive World War II and Charlie's marriage to a conniving heiress. Their story is continued in *One for the Gods* and *Forth Into Light.*

HORMONE PIRATES OF XENOBIA AND **DREAM STUDS OF KAMA LOKA,** by Ernest Posey. These two science-fiction novellas have it all: pages of alien sex, erotic intrigue, the adventures of lunarian superstuds, and the lusty explorations of a graduate student who takes part in his professor's kinky dream project.